P9-BYG-301

A Job for Jenny

Also by Faith Baldwin
in Large Print:

District Nurse
The Heart Remembers
No Bed of Roses
Evening Star
Arizona Star
The Office-Wife
Face Toward the Spring
Rich Girl, Poor Girl
Innocent Bystander
The Rest of My Life With You
That Man is Mine
"Something Special"

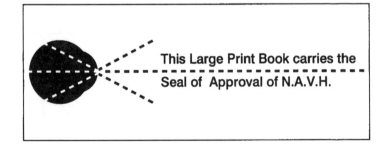

This Large Print Book carries the
Seal of Approval of N.A.V.H.

A Job for Jenny

FAITH BALDWIN

F
Bald

Thorndike Press • Thorndike, Maine

9/97   Thorndike   19.95

Published in 1997 by arrangement with
Harold Ober Associates Inc.

Thorndike Large Print ® Candlelight Series.

The tree indicium is a trademark of Thorndike Press.

The text of this Large Print edition is unabridged.
Other aspects of the book may vary from the original edition.

Set in 16 pt. Plantin by Minnie B. Raven.

Printed in the United States on permanent paper.

Library of Congress Cataloging in Publication Data

Baldwin, Faith,   1893–
    A job for Jenny / Faith Baldwin.
        p.   cm.
    ISBN 0-7862-1185-7 (lg. print : hc : alk. paper)
    1. Large type books.   I. Title.
[PS3505.U97J6   1997]
813´.52—dc21   97-21451

For Two Birthdays —

HERVEY'S AND ANN'S

WITH LOVE.

Chapter One

Jenny shot out of the house and down the walk. She heard Gram calling after her, "Have you a clean handkerchief?" shouted back, "Two of 'em," and proceeded on her way. The little gate squeaked, stuck as usual, and she gave it a violent shove which nearly removed it from its protesting hinges. She thought, tearing down the street, Gram's like Mrs. March in *Little Women*, and chuckled. She was, she calculated, a minute and a half late for the bus.

She turned the corner on, so to speak, one wheel, and there it was, just shoving off. She yelled, "Hi" and the bus groaned and stopped. Passengers craned their necks, and the bus driver grinned. The passengers settled down again. It was just little Jenny Newton, making the bus again, by the skin of her pretty teeth. . . .

She climbed on, hatless, breathless. Her short, slightly shabby tweed skirt of prewar vintage, displayed excessively good legs. The spring sun was tangled in her curly red hair. Her face was rosy with exertion, her blue eyes smiling and relieved. The bus driver prophesied, kindly, "Jenny, one of these days, when you do a Dagwood, you're going to break your neck."

"Okay," said Jenny cheerfully, "so I'll break it, and you can take up a collection among the passengers and send lilies. Gosh, Mac, I haven't any change!"

"As usual," said Mac, with resignation. But resignation was not all he felt when he looked at Jenny. He was this side of forty, and had a good wife, but she weighed one hundred and eighty-six pounds and suffered from allergies. Jenny weighed about one hundred and ten, dripping wet, and apparently she could eat anything. She was twenty years old and Mac had known her for at least three-quarters of her lively life. Before the increased pace of the Seahaven shipyard, together with gas restriction on private cars, had brought Mac's lumbering bus into being, he had driven a taxi and many a time he had been called to the Newton house.

He gave Jenny her change. He asked, "How's the job?" and she looked at him and smiled. She said, "It's wonderful!" and Mac thought, Jeeze, what a kid . . . she wears out her fingernails at a typewriter in the yard her old man used to own and she says it's wonderful!

Jenny stumbled happily to a vacant place. It wasn't very vacant but two large gentlemen made a sliver of room for her. She was no angel, it was doubtful that she could stand on the head of a pin, but her bodily structure was streamlined to fit small spaces.

The majority of the people in the bus intimated that they were aware of her presence. They waved, or smiled, or nodded and some of them spoke. Some said, "Jenny . . . how's tricks?" and a good-looking girl across the aisle raised her voice over the subdued roar of the engine, and said, "Tell Ede to call me up someday. I haven't seen her for weeks."

Jenny nodded, and then scowled slightly. The good-looking girl was Agnes Simpson. Ede was Jenny's older sister. Only last week Ede had spent an afternoon with Agnes and had come home to narrate the events of the day in detail, to Jenny and Gram.

Jenny shrugged. She gave up. Agnes, despite her new husband, and newer baby, was as scatterbrained is she had been when she and Ede were in High together, giggling in the Newton back yard or slurping up sodas at the Busy Corner. Time probably meant nothing to Agnes. She was a lucky creature. Her husband was not only attractive but 4-F.

Jenny looked out the windows. There wasn't a street in Seahaven she didn't know; not a corner, not a turn, not a road, and hardly a house. She had been born in the town, which meant close to the sea. Born, her grandmother said, in a storm, the worst autumn storm in years. Her mother's fragile young life had gone out with the tide that October morning and ten years later Jenny's father had died in another storm, washed off the deck of a small fishing boat. . . .

Seahaven was an old town. The bus was turning away from the residential section now, leaving the wide, tree-bordered streets with the strips of violet-starred grass between sidewalk and road, into the narrower, crooked business section. All the roads led to the sea. Seahaven smelled always of the sea, of wet, rotting timber, of new shavings and of fish. Today it smelled of spring, for the lilacs were coming into flower and presently it would be Decoration Day and the country club would open . . . and after that summer would come in, blue and gold and green and the white beaches would be crowded with youngsters and the sun would sparkle on the little waves and you could almost forget the war. . . .

Passing Canton Street, Jenny looked out

and saw Dr. Barton's car parked outside one of the little white frame houses. Canton Street was paved with blocks brought from China in the clipper ship days. The Seahaven yard had built notable clippers. They had had great designers, great captains. They had competed in the tea races, sailing from Pagoda Anchorage, nine miles below the city of Foochow, where the branches of the yellow Min unite. Gram never let Jenny and Ede forget the clipper days. Nor could they, if they wished, for the square white house in which they lived, with the orchard behind and the wide green lawn in front, was topped with a square structure known as the Captain's Walk or, more grimly, Widow's Walk. And the Newtons had always been shipbuilders and seafarers.

The big man sitting next to Jenny spoke to her, putting his paper aside. He worked at the yard, too, in the personnel department. He said, "We're going to miss you."

She reminded him, smiling, "I'm just moving upstairs."

"This is your first day, isn't it?"

"That's right," said Jenny. Her heart thumped. She was so excited she wanted to get out and walk, run, fly. She wanted to push down walls. She wanted to shout. But she kept her voice down, she restrained her impulse to beat the gentleman from personnel upon his broad back and demand, "Isn't it marvelous? As of today, I'm Justice Hathaway's secretary!"

Secretary to the shipyard manager, who was also the owner's son; her own small private office next to his office, which was paneled in fine wood and appropriately decorated with old prints of clippers and little ship models; a raise in pay; and best of all, the feeling that she would be more a part of things than she had been in her routine work as secretary to the personnel manager.

It isn't, she told herself severely, that he's the best-looking man I've ever seen. At least, not entirely.

The man next to her asked, "Think you'll like it?"

"Sure," said Jenny, "I'll be crazy about it. It isn't as if I didn't know something about the job. Remember last winter when Miss Granley was ill, and I took over for two weeks?"

He said, "Well, good luck. Come down and see us sometime, won't you?"

The bus made a special shipyard stop, as did all the other buses. The Seahaven shipyard was very busy, these days, building small, fast, deadly craft for the Navy. Production had stepped up, a thousand per cent, and the yard had been enlarged. People from all over the state had poured in to find employment there. That was one trouble, Jenny thought, you no longer knew everybody.

She, and a dozen others, got out at the yard, passed the guard, showing their badges, packages or lunch boxes. The guard peered solemnly into Jenny's handbag. He said, "You girls carry the damnedest truck."

He always said it. Someday she'd astonish him and present for his inspection a bag as neat as Gram's remarkable reticule. She would have special places for powder and lipstick, handkerchief and cleansing tissues, change, bills and cigarettes. The guard would faint.

She was still smiling when she reached the private offices in the old red-brick building. They had been redecorated when Horace Hathaway, smelling war, smelling, perhaps, profits, had come up from New York and bought the Goddard-Newton yard . . . then somnolent in the sun, employing only a handful of men, building little fishing boats and not much else, its past glory and prosperity only a memory in Seahaven.

That had been four years ago.

Jenny walked into the anteroom to the manager's office. The manager's departing

13

secretary, Charlotte Granley, was still there and would be until noon. Charlotte had joined the WAVES and Jenny envied her. But Jenny couldn't join the WAVES or any other branch of the service. She had to stay with Gram.

There was no one in the anteroom. Jenny went to the windows and looked down on the wonderful, exciting activities of the yard and at the bright blue water beyond. When she had first come here to work, two years ago, Gram had been unhappy about it. Tradition decreed that Newtons owned the shipyard, they did not pound typewriters in them, under an alien direction and ownership.

The door to the secretary's office opened and Charlotte Granley stood there, and smiled. She said, "Hello, Miss Newton . . . I thought I heard you come in."

Jenny said guiltily, "I'm three minutes late. And I thought I'd be here early. But I missed the early bus and darned near the second. I —" she yawned frankly — "I overslept. Spring or something."

She looked at Charlotte with admiration. Charlotte was tall and slender. Her molasses-colored hair was dressed high, and sleek. She wore a beautifully tailored black suit and impeccable make-up. If her stockings weren't nylon Jenny would eat them.

She was conscious of her tweed skirt, the small, worn brogues, her sweater. Not that she didn't look all right in a sweater. Not like Ede, of course, but then Ede was the family beauty. Still, I'll get by, thought Jenny.

She looked at Charlotte, chuckled and shook her red head.

"What's funny?" inquired Charlotte in her clipped speech.

"Nothing. Only," said Jenny, "poor Mr. Hathaway . . . we're quite a contrast, aren't we?"

Charlotte bent her shining head. She appreciated the implication and was bitterly amused. She had come to Seahaven with Justice Hathaway four long years ago.

She said, "I should think he would find you quite refreshing."

She watched Jenny take off and hang up her little jacket. She said, "Let's go into Mr. Hathaway's office and go over the routine. I don't think you need me really, as you found your way around very efficiently the two weeks I was away, and with no one to help you except" — she paused — "Mr. Hathaway."

"He wasn't here much," said Jenny, "I sort of went at it on my own. You know, grim determination, hammer and tongs, do or die stuff. He was in Washington once, New York too, and Boston, so there were days when I didn't see him at all. But I managed. Newton luck, I guess."

Charlotte said slowly, "You must have managed, because he asked for you when I resigned. I had thought — one of the girls from the Hathaway Boston or New York office but, he said, you knew the job."

"Well," said Jenny, "I don't know about that. I do know the shipyard — I was brought up in it, practically."

"I see," said Charlotte absently. Then her cool, turquoise eyes widened. *"Newton?"* she repeated. "That Newton?"

"Roger," said Jenny. "The Newtons and the Goddards built the yard and all the ships that were launched here. Clippers, sailing ships, and then steam. Yachts too, some of which sailed against Lipton. But, came the crash and all that. People stopped buying yachts and cruisers. My grandfather had already sold part of his half to the Goddards, and then my father sold his share. And the Goddards finally sold to Mr. Hathaway."

"I see," said Charlotte again. Then she said briskly, "Shall we take a look at the files? I dare say you'll turn 'em around. Everyone, no matter what system they've been taught,

16

evolves their own."

The polished Miss Granley and Jenny spent a busy morning. Before the lunch hour arrived Charlotte sat down in the big chair back of the big desk and waved Jenny to the one opposite. She said, "You needn't look reluctant. Justice — that is, Mr. Hathaway, won't be in before late afternoon, if then."

Jenny perched herself on the chair. Charlotte noted that her legs, even in cottons, were excellent. She felt a detached pity for the younger girl. Poor kid, cooped up in this salty little dump, and exposed to Justice's well-known charm . . . Well, it's none of my business, she thought. If I tell her to watch her step she'll think I'm jealous. Maybe I am . . . but not of him . . . that's over, thank God . . . just of her, at twenty, content and not knowing the answers.

Jenny was looking at a picture on the bookcase. She asked, "Is that a new picture of Mrs. Hathaway?"

Charlotte nodded. "It came last week," she said.

Jenny said, "I admired the other pictures very much, when I was here last winter. She's a beautiful woman."

Charlotte said, "I suppose you know that she's been away over four years . . . She was in England when the war broke out. She has

17

relatives there. So she stayed, and later, of course, took the Red Cross job."

Jenny got up and went to the bookcase. Andrea Hathaway had quiet, direct eyes, and a thin, distinguished face. She looked handsome and severe in uniform. On the other end of the bookcase was one of the pictures Jenny had seen last winter. It had been taken ten years ago, on Mrs. Hathaway's wedding day. The same eyes looked at Jenny and smiled. The young face was misted in veiling. The mouth curved.

Jenny asked, "They never had any children, did they?"

"One," said Charlotte. "A boy. He died."

"Oh," said Jenny, "how dreadful!"

Charlotte said nothing. She picked up a fat fountain pen and fidgeted with it. She said abruptly, "Tell me about yourself."

"There isn't much," said Jenny. "I live in an old house, I was born in it and my father before me and his father. There's just my grandmother, my sister and me."

Charlotte said, "I've seen your sister. She's very blonde, isn't she, and pretty?"

"Why, yes," said Jenny. "She's a little older than I. She was working in Boston, as a model, when she met, right after Pearl Harbor, the man she married. He's a captain in the Marines. He wasn't here long after their marriage; he went overseas and has been there ever since."

Charlotte commented, "Mary Hathaway and your sister are — quite friendly."

Jenny shrugged. She said, turning away from the bookcase, "Oh, I don't know. They work together at the Red Cross and Ede's been up at the Hathaway place on several occasions."

"I've heard Mr. Hathaway mention her. Justice, that is."

"Well," said Jenny, "most men do mention her, if they've ever seen her."

Charlotte thought again, It isn't my business. She said, "Yes, of course, she's very striking. I was in Boston a month or so ago on this WAVE business and I saw her walking with Mr. Hathaway, on the Common."

Jenny looked startled. She said, "It couldn't have been Ede. She hasn't been to Boston for at least a year."

"Maybe," agreed Charlotte, "it was someone who looked like her." She added, "I'm surprised she hasn't thought of getting a job. It must be rather dull for her twiddling her thumbs and waiting for her husband to return."

"Oh," said Jenny, laughing, "frankly she wouldn't be too good in the routine work. She can't type. She's a total loss around anything mechanical. Dick wouldn't want her to go into any of the services, even if she wanted to. He's old-fashioned that way. So she does the odd jobs, Red Cross work, bond drives, and canteen . . . She likes it, especially the canteen."

"But you," said Charlotte, "you like it — here?"

Jenny shrugged. "I'd rather be doing something more exciting but I can't leave my grandmother. Ede gets part of Dick's pay, of course, and she has the money he'd saved before he went to war. It isn't too much, but it's enough to contribute to the family finances, dress her and all that. He had a little legacy from his father, you see. His mother lives in California. She wanted Ede to come out there and stay with her and for a time she considered it. But more recently she's said she might as well stay here."

"More recently?" said Charlotte and smiled a little.

And Jenny said, "Why, yes, I — well, gosh, I try to persuade myself that this is part of the war effort and sometimes I succeed. I'd be a Nurse's Aide if I could, and work evenings, but as you know the only hospital is miles away and I simply couldn't make it."

Charlotte looked at her watch. She suggested, "Let's go down to the cafeteria."

They went out of the office, downstairs, across the yard and into the sunny, noisy structure which was a Hathaway addition to the yard. They lined up and took their trays and, for one person who knew Charlotte, twenty knew Jenny. When they finally sat down at one of the big scrubbed tables Charlotte said, "You seem to be Miss Shipyard of 1943."

"Well, gosh," said Jenny, slightly embarrassed, "I've grown up with a lot of the people who worked here or else —"

"Or else they worked for your grandfather?" concluded Charlotte.

She regarded Jenny's well-filled tray and sighed. With Jenny's figure and youth and metabolism, she could probably eat anything and as much of it as she wished. Charlotte's austere meal consisted of a slice of whole wheat bread, no butter, a salad, and a glass of milk.

She asked curiously, "What do you find to do in a place like this? Not that I haven't lived here for four years but I still wonder."

"Oh," said Jenny, "I get around. Of course, with most of the boys gone it's not as lively as it used to be."

"How about the love life?"

Jenny said, "I play the field."

"At your age? You're learning young,"

Charlotte commented.

"That's why," said Jenny in triumph. "I think Ede made a mistake. Not that Dick Ainslee isn't a swell person. But she knew him only a few weeks before she came barging in with him and told Gram they were going to be married, at once, and in the best parlor. And then they had such a short time together before he went away. I suppose it's natural," she said, "but it doesn't make much sense."

"Do you mean to tell me that you haven't anyone special?"

Jenny shook her head. "Nope," she said.

She thought of Steve. Steve Barton. Dr. Steve Barton of the Navy . . . somewhere in the South Pacific until recently; and now in a West Coast hospital with a badly damaged right hand. She thought, I'll go around and see Uncle Bert tonight.

Charlotte thought, That's bad. Justice is bad for any girl who hasn't anyone "special." Even for those who have. She isn't, of course, his type, and that's a break for her, in one way, although she may suffer a few heartaches because of it. But not as many as if she were . . .

How long for herself? Six years. When Andrea Hathaway went abroad, and when she notified her husband that she intended to remain, Charlotte had been happier than ever before, or since, in her life. Surely he would see that his wife intended to leave him, for good . . . in spirit, if not in letter. Surely he would ask her for a divorce . . . even if his pompous old father didn't approve of divorce and did approve of his daughter-in-law?

He hadn't.

She was over it now and for keeps. She admitted to herself that she hadn't joined up from any deep-rooted patriotic motive, merely from a desire to get away — an escape into discipline, regimentation, a sort of anonymity . . . an escape not from Justice Hathaway, but from herself, and from the years she had been with him.

Jenny said, "Gosh, that was good."

She smiled. It was like a child smiling, open, warm, friendly. When Jenny smiled she was very nearly beautiful. When she was extremely grave or extremely angry she was wholly so. The rest of the time she was simply one of the prettiest, most natural girls you've ever seen.

Charlotte looked at her and her heart tightened with the old apprehension. Silly of it, as nothing mattered now, yet it was a habit you couldn't break yourself of, easily, as they are the habits of the senses . . . your eyes cannot look upon a face once desperately beloved, nor your ears hear a voice once magically compelling, without communicating it to your nerves.

She said suddenly, "I wish you lots of luck in the new job."

"I'll need it," said Jenny, "although the two weeks I substituted for you he seemed awfully easy to work for. I made a lot of goofy mistakes and he was very decent about them."

"He isn't hard to work for," said Charlotte evenly, "if you don't mind his tearing off to parts unknown every so often, or keeping you overtime or sending for you to come up to the house . . ."

"That," said Jenny, "should be fun. A break in the monotony anyway."

Charlotte's brightly painted mouth quivered slightly. It wasn't exactly a smile. She said remotely, "Working for Justice is never monotonous."

Chapter Two

They went back to the office after lunch and Charlotte collected her things. She looked through the desk in her former office, and found it neat, and impersonal. She went back to the big office where Jenny was trying to make friends with the files and regarded the desk and the chair and the walls. She looked at the clipper ship models and at the photographs of Mrs. Hathaway and tried to believe that she would never see any of these things, nor this room, nor Justice again.

The door opened and he came in. She hadn't expected him. She had hoped she need not see him.

"Hello, you two," he said. He smiled at Jenny. "Charlotte tell you the worst?" he asked.

Jenny's heart performed a nip-up. It wasn't decent for any man to be so good-looking . . . The old cliché. Tall, dark, handsome. Only very superlative, all three. Every girl was usually a little in love with her boss even if he wasn't as super as this one. She thought, I bet Charlotte was . . . maybe she still is. She thought, further, And I am too — a little . . . ever since last winter . . . or even before, when he used to buzz in and out of the personnel office.

She said, smiling in return, "Miss Granley's been very kind."

"Kindness," said Justice, "is one of her outstanding characteristics, together with generosity." He looked at Charlotte. He asked, "Did you tell her what an ogre I am? Dracula and Frankenstein's monster in a pleasant but lethal blend?"

"Of course," said Charlotte gravely, "as only a heel would shove a child into traffic without explaining the lights."

Justice's heavy brows drew together and there was open hostility in his regard. Jenny felt uneasy. She thought, What gives? The air was tense with something too intimate and angry for ordinary dislike between employer and employee.

Charlotte said, "Well, it's time to shove off." She smiled, adding, "Extraordinary how nautical one becomes, so soon." She looked at Justice. "I'm sorry," she said, "not to have seen Mary again."

That was to annoy him. Charlotte Granley had had very little to do with Justice's younger sister, and she had never called her by her first name — except, of course, to Justice.

"She'll be devastated," he said. "Here, let me walk to the corridor with you."

Jenny waited. She thought, I bet she *was* in love with him. I bet she was fired. She looked at Mrs. Hathaway's newest picture, again. She thought, How in the world a woman could go off and leave a man like this even if there is a war on . . . ?

When Justice came back, his face was flushed and a brooding sort of melancholy darkened it. But, looking at Jenny, his expression cleared. He said: "Well, that's that. Great girl, Charlotte. I suppose we should put up a service star."

He looked at Jenny with sudden defiance, as if she had spoken, and added, "I suppose you wonder why I'm not in it? Well, I'd like to be. But I can't. My father, who has a dozen other interests, scattered all over the face of the country, took it upon himself to buy a shipyard. Then he decided he was too busy to run it. He bought himself a place up here but rarely lives in it. He attends the directors' meetings and that's about all. He dumped the whole works in my lap. So I'm classed as essential. It's a wonderful world. My sister runs canteens and labors at the Red Cross and antagonizes the hell out of a

27

town which won't admit you live here until one day they discover you've been here forty years and are about to die. My secretary becomes a sailor, my wife barges around England in a uniform, survives blitzes, breaks her arm in a blackout, runs a string of service clubs, and I sit here and —" He broke off. "Sorry," he said. "I forgot that I don't know you very well."

"That's all right," said Jenny. "Now I feel that I know you better."

His face cleared and he laughed. "Sit down. How old are you?"

"Twenty."

"Yes. I remember now — but you look about fourteen. Your sister —" he hesitated a moment — "she's older, isn't she?"

"Four years," said Jenny. She looked at him, her very blue eyes clear and friendly. She said, "I keep forgetting you met her last autumn when the special Red Cross classes met up at the Elton — I mean your place."

She was scarlet.

"See what I mean?" he demanded. "We've lived in that house four years, added wings, stables, a swimming pool and enough landscaping for a summer resort and people like you still call it the Elton place!"

Jenny sat very erect. She said, with spirit: "You needn't get sore about it, Mr.

Hathaway. It's been the Elton place for a couple of hundred years. Maybe more. I used to go there when I was a youngster. Ede practically grew up there. One of the Eltons used to design yachts for us, and several of them were clipper captains. After all, the bank only took over about eight years ago, and it was boarded up until you came along."

"I apologize," he said instantly. "Perhaps, in another two hundred years, it will be known as Hathaway Harbor, or something. I should live so long! Ede . . . that's your sister's name isn't it?"

"Well, Edith really, after our mother," said Jenny.

"She's very attractive," he went on. "Has she heard from her husband lately?"

"She hears irregularly," said Jenny, "lots of letters — then gaps. You know how it is . . . he's on one of those dreadful little islands."

Justice said absently, "Too bad." Then he picked up a folder and looked through it. He asked, "What did you tell me your name was — your first named?"

"Jenifer," she said. "There's always been a Jenifer Newton, well, most always. There was a clipper ship named that . . . the *Jenifer Newton*. No one ever calls me that except

Gram and she does only when she's mad at me."

"Often?"

"Odd Tuesdays," said Jenny gravely.

He said, "I'll call you Jenny, whether I'm mad at you or not. Odd Wednesdays, shall we say, for my fits of anger. Too bad to have it hang over you on the same day . . . I've never liked a formal office. Now, do you think you can take some letters for me?"

"If I can't," said Jenny — "and I could last winter, you may remember . . . Mr. John R. Gregg would be very much astonished, not to say, miffed."

She crossed her feet at the ankles and waited. Her heart kept on doing little acrobatics. It was spring, and spring was always exciting. The yard hummed all around them, and the sun was unseasonably warm for the middle of May. But the old brick building was cool. Jenny wasn't. Jenny was a child going to her first party, Jenny was a kid, tearing into the drugstore for a soda, Jenny was a girl in an apple orchard being kissed for the first time. Well! But *that* was Steve and Steve kissed her often, absent-mindedly, carelessly, fraternally, and then, when he went away to war, hard and long. But that was just because he was going.

Dear Steve, she thought, making her pothooks, he was wonderful — laughing and gay and as excited about things as she was, an idealist, with a sense of humor, a marvelous friend . . . He was a good doctor. He was going to be a remarkable surgeon . . . or, she corrected herself sadly, he would have been if that Jap bomb hadn't landed on the dressing station . . .

"Read that back, will you?" asked Justice.

She read it back. He leaned forward in his chair and grinned. He said, "I thought I'd catch you. You had a — faraway look."

"I'm purely a robot," said Jenny serenely. "I can write your letters and still think my own thoughts."

He said, "I think I'm going to like having you here, Jenny," and went on dictating. But, much later, when the last letter was inscribed in the notebook he asked carelessly:

"You and your sister aren't much alike, are you?"

"Why, no," said Jenny, giving the question her attention, "I don't think so. For one thing, she's better-looking and for another — well, our dispositions are rather different."

"How?" asked Justice.

Jenny shook her head. "I don't know . . . I mean, in order to understand you'd have to know us both . . . I've always claimed mine was better."

"I see," said Justice, and rose. He added, "I won't be back today. I'll sign those in the morning. Good-bye, till then."

He smiled at her, from the door. She thought, Whoops! She looked over at the bookcase, rose, collected her notebook and betook herself to her own small office. Mustn't forget the gentleman has a wife. But a wife who doesn't get home once in four years doesn't seem very real somehow, doesn't really rate. She thought, with hopefulness, Maybe they're separated . . . I mean actually separated but not saying anything about it.

Wife or no wife, separated or not, she was a little in love with Justice Hathaway. Not hurtingly, nor demandingly so, just — with excitement. It was fun. It was interesting. She told herself, putting the paper in the typewriter, Jenny, watch your impulses. Gram would have your ears if she knew the things you think!

Chapter Three

When Jenny walked home from the bus stop, the spring dusk was cool and blue. The gate in the little picket fence still stood crooked, as she had left it that morning. The old apple trees on either side of the square white house bent gnarled, mothering arms, feathered with green. Soon they and the orchard in the back yard would foam up in coral and white.

The lawn was ragged. In a little while it should be cut. Whenever will I have time? thought Jenny. Ede won't . . . maybe we can hire some kid, after school.

She went up the walk to the steps. The second was broken. You always had to remember that. Her shoes clattered on the wooden boards of the porch and she opened the door and went in. The door was never locked.

Jenny spun through the living room and dining room, which were big and cluttered and pleasant. On the other side of the wide hall were the best parlor and the library. They were aired and dusted regularly but no one used them, or hardly ever.

Gram was in the kitchen. Gram was Mrs. Henry Newton, born Emily Adams. Gram was little, thin as a bird and as spry. She was over seventy. She had white, thickly curling hair, which had once been as red as Jenny's. She wore it short as Jenny's, ever since her bout with pneumonia three years ago. Jenny had never known another mother or another home. The thing she envied Ede for most was that Ede claimed she could remember their mother. But Jenny had always argued, "You couldn't, you were only four!"

Gram was stirring a pot of her wonderful split pea soup. She asked, "Late, aren't you?"

"Not very. I worked like anything. After all, it was my first day."

"How did it go?"

"I was a marvel of efficiency. Mr. Hathaway said he had never seen anyone like me before. He offered me a place on the board of directors and two thousand dollars a month," said Jenny modestly.

Gram said, "You're an idiot. Go along and wash up and see if Ede is ready. She came in long ago and I asked her to set the table, but she hasn't put in an appearance."

Jenny put her arm around Gram's thin shoulders and squeezed hard. She said,

"Isn't everything wonderful? Better job, raise, spring coming and maybe Steve will be coming home. I'll whip around and see Uncle Bert tonight —"

She went out of the kitchen on the double. It was difficult for the younger Miss Newton to walk sedately. She went upstairs, her hand light on the lovely wood of the banister polished by many hands, over many years. She yelled, "Ede, soup's on and why didn't you set the table?" and went into her own room. She loved her room. It was big and shabby and the chintz was faded. It was untidy but very clean. Gram and the cleaning woman saw to the cleanliness. The untidiness was Jenny's idea.

Jenny's tiger cat sat in the middle of Jenny's big four-poster bed. Her name was Burning Bright, and so they called her Butch. She was about to have kittens. Sooner or later, no matter what anyone did about it, she would have them on Jenny's bed.

Butch purred. "Oh, you!" said Jenny disdainfully, "you can't pull the wool over my eyes. In the cellar for you tonight. Knock if you need me . . ."

She went into the bathroom, whisked out again and was combing her hair at the dresser mirror, ornamented with snapshots of a dozen boys in uniform, and especially with snapshots of Dr. Stephen Barton, when Ede strolled in.

Ede was a honey. Ede was quite a dish. Brown eyes, pale-blonde hair, a very fair skin. Her features were much better than Jenny's. They were close to classic. But her red mouth drooped at the corners and she had restless, secret eyes.

Taller than Jenny, her figure was perfect. It was her figure and also her dislike of the life Seahaven offered that had sent her, greatly against Gram's wishes, to Boston, and the big dress shop.

She asked, "How did things go?"

Jenny turned. She said, "Gram asked me, now you. How should they go? They went wonderfully. I am practically the best secretary in the state."

Ede smiled. "Charlotte Granley wouldn't like to hear you say that."

"I didn't know you even knew each other," said Jenny.

"I don't, really," said Ede. "She was up at the Hathaway place one day when I was there."

"Well, she's gone to be an admiral or something," said Jenny, "and the big shot will have to make do with me. Ede, you've met him — he asked about you today —

don't you think he's *terribly* good-looking?"

"Oh, sure," said Ede, "by Seahaven standards . . . He asked about me," she added, "what?"

"Just, how you were, and had you heard from Dick," said Jenny vaguely. She rose. She said, to the cat, "Butch, don't you dare deliver while I'm at supper — and I have an engagement afterwards, remember."

"You ought to get rid of that cat," said Ede, as they went out into the hall together, "you're always racing around helping her have kittens, and then finding a home for them."

"Steve gave her to me," said Jenny, "when she was just a kitten and cute as a bug. I don't care how many kittens she has. That's her nature, poor dear."

Ede said, "Tolerant, aren't you? What about Steve?"

"I don't know any more than you do," said Jenny, "but I wish he'd come home soon. It's going to be swell having him around again."

"I'm not so sure," said Ede, "for him . . . after all, he hadn't planned to come back here and go into general practice. He'd planned to be a surgeon."

Gram called, "Girls — are you ready?" and Jenny whispered, "She's not feeling affectionate, Ede. She did ask you to set the table."

"I'm sorry," said Ede, "I started manicuring my nails — though why I bother trying new shades in this place I wouldn't know — and forgot."

At supper Jenny sat, frowning, a forkful of corned beef suspended in mid-air. She asked presently, "Ede, what was that about Mary Hathaway? I'm trying to remember and can't. Didn't we hear she'd been engaged or something?"

"She was," said Ede, "and the invitations were out and then it was called off."

"I wonder why," asked Jenny. "I haven't seen her more than two or three times, but she's very attractive."

Gram said, "Gossip . . ."

"Not really, I remember now, it was in the papers," Jenny defended herself.

Gram said. "Every woman is permitted to change her mind. Your mother was engaged before she met your father."

"Well, for heaven's sake!" said Jenny. "She was? Who to?"

"If your grammar is as careless," said Gram, "in your work, I wonder Mr. Hathaway selected you from all the other secretaries."

"Oh," said Jenny, "that's all right. At home I take off mental and linguistic corsets. To whom, darling?" she asked politely.

"To Bert Barton."

Jenny dropped her fork and Ede gasped. They cried, with one voice, "No one ever told me!"

"It never came up before," said Gram. "Your mother met your father again — he had been away from Seahaven for some time — and that was that. Bert was very unhappy about it, but after all he was a good deal older than herself. Then he met Sarah in Providence, and married her. You don't remember her, do you?"

"I do too," said Jenny indignantly; "she didn't die until I was seven or eight. She was beautiful, and she made the best cookies!"

She rose presently, cleared away, and brought in the stewed rhubarb and cupcakes. She said, dreamily, "I wonder why Justice Hathaway's wife stays away from home . . ."

Ede put down her spoon. She said, "Jenny, you're crazy tonight. All you do is wonder."

"It's a free country," said Jenny, "and I think it's funny, just the same!"

Chapter Four

After the dishes had been cleared, after Jenny and Gram had washed them, as Ede had too much respect for her new polish, Jenny went upstairs to change. She put her head in at Ede's door. Ede was writing letters at the old maple desk. Her pale-gold hair glowed under the light, she looked very young and lonely and Jenny's heart ached for her. She asked, "Want to walk around to Bartons with me?"

"I guess not," said Ede. She turned, and smiled. She added, "I'm going to finish my letter and mail it and then go down to the drugstore and see if there's a book I haven't read. I forgot to go to the lending library."

"Okay," said Jenny, " 'bye."

"Give my love to Uncle Bert," said Ede. "I hope the news of Steve is good."

A little later, after putting Butch in the cellar, Jenny left the house, went down the street, turned the corner and walked for another block. The wind was cool, and a new moon hung, silver, in the dark sky. At the Bartons', a green light burned over the lovely door. The house was nearly a replica of the Newtons', even to the Captain's Walk. The doctor's office had a separate entrance and, looking through an unshaded window, Jenny could see that a patient, an elderly man, waited in the reception room. So she went in at the back door to the kitchen where the doctor's housekeeper sat at the scrubbed table, reading.

"Hi, Mattie," said Jenny, "is Uncle Bert going out after office hours?"

Mattie took off her glasses. She was sixty years old and looked like a slightly frost-bitten apple. She doubled in brass as receptionist and message taker since the office nurse had joined the Army Nurse Corps. She said:

"No one's called him yet, Jenny, and I hope to the Lord they won't. He ain't well. I'm worried about him. He's been to see Dr. Mathews twice to my knowledge, not that he'd come right out and tell me. I've been so worried I even wrote Steve. Now I wish I hadn't, as he has enough on his plate, poor boy."

Jenny sat down by the table and reached absently for a hot doughnut which, with a dozen others, were on a blue plate on the table.

"Have you heard from Steve?" she asked,

41

"since he telephoned?"

"Yes," said Mattie, "he's coming home. Not that I wanted anything to happen to the boy," she said unnecessarily, "but since it had to happen, and wasn't too bad, thank God, now maybe he'll settle down and take some of the burden off his father's shoulders."

Jenny drew a deep breath. "Just how bad is it?" she asked. "Uncle Bert wasn't sure . . . last time I saw him."

"The hand's stiff," said Mattie, "two fingers are bent. They're doing things for it."

"Will it always be stiff?" Jenny asked anxiously. She added, "It's his *right* hand!"

"I know," said Mattie. "Steve's heart is set on surgery and he won't get over this easy. But it can't be helped."

She put her glasses back on her nose.

"How's your grandma?" she asked.

They talked of Gram, and Ede, Ede's husband, of the shipyard and, presently, of Jenny's new job. "They say," said Mattie, "that half the Hathaway servants left but Mary Hathaway brought new help up from New York. Not that they'll last any longer than the rest," she added.

They heard, presently, slow, heavy footsteps and Dr. Barton put his head in at the door. "Hello, Jenifer," he said, "gossiping, you girls?"

"I came to see you, too," she told him. "Twice, lately I've been in and you weren't here. Gram says, when are you coming to dinner?"

"Ask Mattie when I have time to eat." He sat down on a kitchen stool, said, "Give me a doughnut," and Mattie rose, went to the icebox and returned with a glass of milk. She said, "He had to go out during supper and never did finish eating."

"And I shouldn't be eating this," said Dr. Barton, biting into the doughnut with appreciation.

He was a very big man, and had taken on weight in the last few years. He had a large head and a great shock of white hair. His face was brown and lined. He was Mattie's age but looked older. Under the darkness of his skin there was a gray pallor that frightened Jenny.

"You're working too hard," she said.

"Oh, sure," said Barton, "and who isn't? There's not a young man left, as you well know, Jenny. Mathews, Brown, and I have to take on all Seahaven and the outlying rural districts. We haven't enough nurses, and as for getting patients into the Northam hospital, it's damned near impossible."

"Don't swear, doctor," said Mattie mildly, as she always did. He grinned, and ignored her, as usual.

"Mathews," he said, "is a G.P. But he's even older than I am, which makes him Methuselah. Brown's a surgeon, and has more than he can do. Of course, there's Peters, but he specializes . . . or did — now he doesn't, as much."

He sighed. He added, "When Steve comes home —"

"When will that be?" asked Jenny. "Mattie says you've heard from him again."

"I don't know the date. I've had just one letter from him since the phone call, and he's still in the hospital in California . . . I gave you the address. Have you written him?"

"Of course," said Jenny, "but he hasn't answered."

Steve's father sighed again. He said, "It isn't like him but he's taking this hard. He can't be a surgeon now, and that's all he ever wanted to be since the days he used to catch frogs at Basset Pond and dissect them in the bathroom."

He coughed, and flushed with the effort. He rose from the stool and set his glass down on the table. "Come into the office, Jenifer," he said, "and talk, although you and Mattie have doubtless exhausted all the really good scandal. How's everyone at home?"

"Fine," said Jenny, following him out of the kitchen. "Gram's sprier than I am, and Ede's all right. Only, of course, not very happy."

"Who in thunder is, nowadays?" demanded Dr. Barton, "except healthy infants who cannot understand the conversation, anxieties and sorrows of their elders — to say nothing of their neuroses — and who, by the same token, can't read. Come in, and sit down."

The office was big, with many windows. There was an old couch across one wall and by the fireplace the doctor's cluttered desk, his vast chair and the facing chair, for patients. Books crowded the shelves and the room was permeated with a faint scent of tobacco and medicine. It was a comfortable and shabby room, the fireplace blackened with the smoke of innumerable fires. The examining room beyond was bright with metal and very modern. But the office had been the same for as long as Jenny could remember and for years before that.

"Mind if I lie down?" asked Barton, and lowered his bulk to the couch, grunting slightly. He punched at a pillow and wadded it under his head. He added apologetically, "Have to go out tonight, probably."

Jenny turned the big chair to face him and

sat down in it. She did not like his color, nor his look of strain. She said gently, "You're pretty tired."

"Me and everyone else," he answered, and smiled at her. "Don't worry."

"Steve will."

He drew his heavy brows together. "I suppose so," he answered. "Normally I'd try to keep him from it — but perhaps it will be good for him."

"Why?" asked Jenny.

"His hand," said Barton. "Oh, there's no use evading it, Jenny. He's very bitter. He had big dreams and they were likely to come true. He's a hard worker, and brilliant. Now he has to resign himself to a routine practice — not only on account of his hand but because of me . . ."

Jenny asked, after a minute, "Are you going to tell me about it?"

"Yes," answered Barton, as if astonished, "I am. I think Steve's fonder of you than of anyone in the world except me. And you can help him more than I. You're a woman, Jenny," he explained, smiling, "and his contemporary, even if he's a decade older. Those ten years made a lot of difference when you were a long-legged little kid and he was in college . . . but not now." He broke off and reached in his pocket for his pipe. Jenny took some matches from the desk and offered them to him but he shook his head. He cradled the cold pipe in his hands and went on: "You know the boy. He's a stubborn fellow. And he feels things deeply. If he had only his hand to worry about, well —" he shrugged — "but now," he added, "he has me, and maybe that's a good thing."

"Why aren't you smoking?" she asked gravely, for he was a prodigious smoker, when, his work over, he could, temporarily, relax.

"Smart girl," he answered. "Only because I've been told not to, my dear."

"It's your heart," said Jenny flatly.

"Yup," he said heavily. "Damned thing got tired, dragging me around. I saw Mathews, then I sneaked off to Boston and consulted a cardiac man. But he couldn't do much more than confirm Mathews's diagnosis — and my own, I'm not too dumb, you know. So, I have to ease off. Hell, I asked him, how am I supposed to do that with most of the profession gone to war? Civilians still get sick. So he gave me my choice. Said I could keep on driving myself and live for a while or taper off and live perhaps my allotted span, whatever that is. So I picked the short life. What else could I do? But now the picture's changed. Steve is coming back, he'll take over and I'll rust, quietly." He broke off and looked at her. "What a damned fool I am! Jenny . . . I'm sorry . . ."

She wiped the tears from her face with the back of her hand as a child would. She said, "Don't mind me, Uncle Bert, it was a — shock, that's all."

"I'm pretty selfish," he murmured, "but, you understand, not on my own account. Not that it isn't pleasant to have a pretty girl cry over me, at my age. I told you because of Steve. I want you to help him. I haven't told anyone. Only Mathews knows, and a couple of my old cronies, but no one else. Your grandmother will get it out of me sooner or later, she's always ferreted her way into my secrets. But she'll keep her own counsel, as you will."

"Have you told Steve?" asked Jenny.

"I wrote him, the other day, but I haven't heard yet. If he thinks he can help me, if he believes he'll prolong my time, he'll worry less over his own disability. He'll feel he's to be of some use, after all, no matter how hard the adjustment may be. And he'll do a fine job, my girl. Thank God, he had his full two years, interning, before he went." He put the short pipestem between his strong, discolored teeth and gripped it as if it were a comfort. Then he put the pipe back in his pocket. "I like to kid myself," he said. "I miss the old stinkpot, Jenny. I don't like the diet they've ordered. I have to think about stairs, too. I don't like it at all. And I tell you, straight, I'd a sight rather take the short way out than this — all the coddling . . . it gripes me . . . but, because of Steve, I can't. He must have an incentive, he must forget himself and this is one way he can do it. I don't like that, either. I feel like a heel."

She said, "You're pretty wonderful."

"I bet you say that to all the boys," he told her, with great affection. He was her godfather, as well as her doctor, and he was also her friend.

The telephone rang and Jenny looked at it with hostility. She watched Barton get up slowly, carefully, cross the room and answer it. She heard the questions he asked and heard him say, "I'll be right over."

He picked up his bag and they went out to the hall together where Mattie waited, his topcoat over her arm. She said, "It ain't too warm out, doctor, you'd better wear this, and your hat too."

"What a woman!" he complained. "I can't get away with anything."

Jenny took Mattie's hard, capable hand and held it to her cheek and smiled. "Good night, Mattie," she said. Mattie belonged to Jenny too. She loved her. In the old days when Jenny was thirteen and in love with Steve, first love, terrifying and exciting and an open secret, she used to come in and sit with Mattie in the kitchen when Steve was home, on the chance that he'd tear in from playing tennis or whatever he was doing and say, "Hi, kid, you still around?" and grin at her, his lopsided grin. Mattie knew. Mattie believed in feeding the lovelorn with cookies and milk, with mint-spiced tea and apple turnovers.

"Drop you off home?" asked Barton.

"I'll walk," she said, and watched him get into the car, so very slowly. Her heart ached. She waved her hand and he said, "I'll call you as soon as I hear from Steve. . . . Hold on, Jenny, come here."

She went close to the window and leaned in.

He said, "I had no business burdening you with this. Forget it if you can. Just stand by Steve, that's all."

The car pulled away and she stood there, quiet and small in the darkness. She heard a boy whistling, and a radio playing. The Harrows had their windows open. She heard a child crying and people laughing, walking up toward her from the corner. She heard the spring wind whispering to the trees and a car went by and then another and she stood there thinking. She thought, I didn't tell him about the new job.

Nothing must happen to Uncle Bert Barton.

Jenny shivered and began walking toward home. Gram would be there, and Ede would be in bed, reading. It would all seem very serene and familiar.

But not quite; there was always the peril and the danger waiting.

She thought, Steve will be home soon.

She had fallen out of love with Steve when she was sixteen and Ham Goddard was captain of the Senior High team. That hadn't lasted long, just long enough to convince her that Steve wasn't the only man in the world. Then she had gone on growing up and the difference in their ages had seemed to lessen and, although Steve was absent from Seahaven so much, they wrote, sporadically, and saw each other when he was home. Jenny had known all about the pretty nurse at M.G.H. and had stood by, with silent sympathy — and, occasionally, expressed impatience — when she married someone else and Steve had sworn that he'd cut his throat. No, damned if he would, he'd live to spite the girl and be the best confounded surgeon in New England . . . he'd serve an assistant apprenticeship with Dr. Holmes, in Boston — see if he didn't make it — and then go ahead, on his own, through with women forever!

Jenny thought, I'm thirsty. The doughnut perhaps. Anyway, she was parched. She was in the Sahara. It was too far to the Busy Corner, but she could cut across and over to the residential end of Canton Street and down a block where there was a neighborhood drugstore, where Ede had gone for her library book. She'd have a soda and talk to old Nat, at the counter.

She walked briskly, meeting few people. At the drugstore, which was almost empty, she perched herself on a stool, ordered a black-and-white, with water for a chaser, and asked Nat, "How's business?"

"Not so hot," he said gloomily, a stooped elderly man with a walrus mustache, "the kids don't come here, like they used to —"

"Why not?" asked Jenny. "They always did . . . It does look deserted tonight, perhaps it's late," she added.

"It ain't late," said Nat, "they run off nowadays to them juke-box places. Got more money than they ever had, to spend, lots of their folks being in defense work. Heck, I don't suppose it matters much, it's more than I can do anyway to wait on all the counters, with the help gone. We're lucky to have a pharmacist left."

He gave Jenny her water and she drank it. "Maybe that's what I wanted most," she said, but when the soda foamed up before her, she seized her straws and absorbed it beatifically. She said, "Ede was in a little while ago for a book, wasn't she?"

"Ain't seen Ede in months," said Nat. "How is she — and what does she hear from her husband?"

Jenny reported on Ede and Dick. She asked for several of the boys who had worked at this counter regularly or on vacations before the war, paid for her soda, bought two movie magazines and some chocolate bars . . . "Is it all right if I take two, Nat, or would you rather I didn't?" . . . and then said good night and went out. Evidently Ede had decided not to get the book.

Going home, the cross-cut way, she saw a car parked by an empty lot, and recognized it. Justice Hathaway was the only person in town with a car like that, long, black, sleek and powerful. She quickened her steps. If Justice were driving and he were alone, he could darned well take her home, she thought happily. But the car started before she reached it and as it pulled away and the street lights shone on it, she saw a pale-gold head, very like Ede's. It couldn't be Ede, however. Perhaps Justice's sister — but not unless she had bleached her hair recently, as she was as dark as Justice.

She thought, Bet it's Charlotte Granley and felt a twinge of envy and annoyance.

When she reached home the porch light was still on and she went into the hall, and snapped it off. Gram called down. She asked, "Is that you, Ede?"

"It's Jenny."

Gram said, "Then don't turn out the light. Ede's still out."

Jenny turned it on again and went upstairs. She went into Gram's room and found her in bed with a book. She sat high, erect, against her pillows with their tatting lace edges, and her white cotton nightgown was ruffled at the neck and wrists, and hand-embroidered. She wore a blue cap on her white curls and silver-trimmed glasses on her nose. She laid aside her book. "Sit down," she said.

Jenny said, "Want I should get you something — glass of milk or a cooky?"

Gram said, "No, thanks, I had a snack, a little while ago. Did you see Bert?"

"Yes . . ."

"What did he say about Steve?"

"He's still in the hospital, but he'll be home soon."

"He said something to upset you," said Gram firmly.

Jenny said, "You'll find out sooner or later, and he didn't make me swear not to tell you. Uncle Bert's sick, Gram. It's his heart. He has to take it easy. If Steve comes home, he'll be able to. He hasn't told anyone but me — and Steve."

Gram's face was suddenly a little whiter, a little thinner. Bert Barton was her good friend, close as a younger brother. She said quietly, "I've suspected as much for some time. Well, there's nothing we can do about it but help where we can. I guess it's up to Steve."

"Yes," said Jenny. She bent and kissed the cool old cheek. She said, "I'll go on to bed now. Here's a couple of magazines for you, and a chocolate bar."

Gram's eyes sparkled. She said scornfully, "That silly stuff!" But she loved the movie magazines, she read them all, she knew more about the stars — more, that is, of publicity released and not suppressed — than Jenny. And she had a passion for chocolate bars.

Jenny dropped the magazines on the bed and Gram said doubtfully, "Well, I'll just look at them, if you don't want them now."

Laughing, Jenny went to her room. She had undressed and was brushing her hair when she heard a car drive up. Her room was at the front of the house, and she ran to look out the window. Justice's car was there and Ede was getting out of it. She stood there talking for a moment. Neither laughed, nor said good night. But Jenny heard her say once, "You promised . . ." and then she seemed to listen, and then there was silence and the car moved away, suddenly noisy, and Ede came slowly up the path. Jenny heard her lock the screen door, and shut the front door. She heard her turn out the porch light, and come upstairs.

Jenny opened her own door and stood there in her pajamas. They were faded, and they had shrunk. They left her ankles bare, and her wrists. They were ridiculous. She had brushed her hair until it shone like copper and curled all over her head. She said imperiously, "Ede, you come here!"

Ede came in. She looked tired. She was wearing, Jenny saw, her prettiest cotton frock, a pale angelic blue, under a little darker blue coat. Her hands were empty, save for a handbag.

Jenny said, "Justice Hathaway brought you home!"

"Well," said Ede mildly, "so what? He was

56

passing, stopped and gave me a lift. Any law against it?"

"No," said Jenny, puzzled, "but you didn't go to Nat's for a book. I stopped in for a soda, and he said you hadn't been there."

"Nat's a goon," said Ede, and yawned. "I went. He was fussing around in the back. I saw Pete — you know, the pharmacist. I didn't find a book I wanted. It was too late to go anywhere else, so I started home and met Mr. Hathaway."

"I saw the car," said Jenny, "it was parked at the corner of Elm and Seabreeze, by the empty lot. I thought I saw you . . . but I didn't believe it, and just as I got there, you drove off."

Ede said, "It was hardly a major crime, darling. Nor were we parked for pleasure, if that's what you suspect. Something went wrong with the dashboard lights and he stopped to see what was the matter. But why I should —"

Jenny said stubbornly, "I heard you say something about a promise . . . what was that about?"

"That," said Ede, "is none of your —" She stopped. "It is, really. I was talking about you. Your raise."

Jenny flushed. She said, "I wish you wouldn't . . . When I was transferred they said there'd be one and there will be, in due time. They have to fill about nine hundred and ninety-nine forms . . . I don't like your horning in."

"Why not?" asked Ede. "You're my sister, aren't you? And his sister is by way of being a fairly good friend of mine. Or isn't a Newton supposed to aspire to a Hathaway association?" She laughed. Her cheeks were as bright as Jenny's, her long eyes brilliant. She said, "Don't be an idiot. All men are alike. If he can get you for the pittance they paid you at personnel, he will. He'll conveniently forget or else Washington will say no, a thousand times no, who is this salty little wench who demands an extra five bucks in her pay envelope? Yet even five bucks would come in very handy, as you well know. This place is a white elephant," said Ede, with passion, "taxes, repairs and all. If only we could sell it and move into a smaller house."

Jenny said, "Ede, I'm sorry, I —"

"Oh, you," said Ede, "you don't dare put yourself forward! I'm not afraid to do it for you. If it weren't that Gram needs what I can give her out of Dick's money, I'd get out, go back to Boston, find a job and a flat . . . of my own. But Gram gets so upset. And when I wrote Dick about it, wondering if there were some way — after all, if I had a job, I could still give Gram money — he had a fit. He wants to think of me here, he said, with my own people, safe. Men!" Her voice broke. She said, "I'm so damned tired of being alone."

Jenny had forgotten Justice Hathaway. She put her arms around Ede. "Don't, dear," she said.

"You don't understand," said Ede, "you couldn't in a hundred years, unless you were in the spot I'm in. It isn't that I don't love Dick. I do — but —" She pulled herself away. "What on earth is that ghastly noise?" she demanded, startled.

Jenny listened. "Good Lord," she said, "it's Butch!"

She flew downstairs, her oversize slippers flapping and her pajamas strange and shrunken. Ede leaned over the banister and watched her. Jenny would be good for as long as it took Butch to deliver herself of how many kittens she was having this time. Ede shrugged and went to her room, her face grave and unhappy.

Chapter Five

Before Decoration Day the lilacs had bloomed and the orchards bore their beautiful burden, coral and pink, rose and white. Jenny, coming into the office early, stood and looked from the windows toward the bright water. She wore a green linen frock, which made her look like a new leaf, and a pixie. Standing there, she thought back to the summers when she and Steve had spent long salt- and sun-drenched hours on Steve's little catboat. It seemed so remote. But now it would come nearer, it would happen again. Steve would come home, and things would be much as they had been. She thought, I can tell him about Justice.

Justice in her thoughts, *Mr. Hathaway* in the office, although only yesterday he had said to her, "For heaven's sake, Jenny, must you be so protocol-conscious? It would be wonderful to have a few people in this place call me by my given name, besides my family."

Steve would understand about Justice, although he would naturally laugh his head off. He would tell her she had spring fever and write, soberly, a prescription. Sulphur and molasses, most likely. Although once, when she had fallen desperately in love with her high school English teacher, he had written, on his father's prescription blank: "one new beau, unmarried, sound in wind and limb and twenty years younger." Because poor Mr. Harrison had a quite satisfactory wife, was forty-odd and a little on the tubercular side. It wasn't his fault that he looked Byronic, if faded, and had a beautiful, moving voice. All the girls were in love with him that year.

Steve was such fun. And had so much sense. But he was always wanting to do something for someone, reform the world, feed the hungry, heal the sick.

He would understand about Justice because he had known Jenny always. I don't ask a thing, she told herself, except to see him and be friends, have him smile at me and say, "Good job, Jenny."

That was all. He wasn't remotely interested in her. Not that she liked admitting it. But, heck, she told herself stoutly, I'm no glamour girl. Why should he be? I believe he was, in Charlotte, once, anyway, if not at the time she resigned. Even if he were interested, there's nothing anyone could do about it — as he had a wife. Her absence didn't make her less Mrs. Hathaway. Anyway, it wasn't like falling in love with an available person, Jenny told herself. It was like falling in love with Gary Cooper, or Clark Gable, or Cary Grant — and Jenny had been a little in love with each of these planetary gentlemen in turn, and all at once, at one time. . . . Of course, she was Justice's secretary, she saw him daily, she breathed the same air, and she knew him well enough to swear mildly when something went wrong, in his presence, but for all the practical designs she had on him, he might as well have been Mr. Cooper. Steve would understand that. No one else would.

I, said Jenny to her interested self, was not cut out for a Home Wrecker . . . And to tell you the truth, I wouldn't want to be.

Yet falling in love with the boss made the work a lot more interesting. Steve would say, "You're a dope." He'd grin. He'd pinch her nose, which she hated. He'd ask, "Why don't you grow up?" He'd probably kiss her, because it was a habit he occasionally indulged. She liked it. She liked Steve. He was her first love and books said you never get over your first love. Even when other loves thumbed a ride in your crazy, eighty-miles-an-hour heart.

She had written Steve again and had, finally, a reply. He said, they'd let him out soon. He said, he didn't know when. He added, it was damned hard to write, but that he could manage and his right hand was not more illegible than his left. Also, he assured her, he was no hero, so she could wash that idea out of what she deemed her mind.

The communal office boy came in. He officiated in several offices, with office boys rationed. He was a tall, slouchy kid, nearly eighteen. He had graduated from High the year before, bright as a button and lazy as a July afternoon. He was a nephew of the last of the original Goddards and his name was Frank Morrison. He answered to the name of Yip. No one knew why.

Yip's job was errand running, wastepaper baskets and odd jobs. When he was eighteen he would go to war. His mother didn't want him to enlist in the services possible at seventeen. So he worked at the yard. He was a friend of Jenny's, she had known him all his life, but lately his efficiency had decreased to the vanishing point. Today he was late. He was sleepy. His hair was on end. He had a slight, but perceptible down on his upper lip, and his usually clear skin was murky, his eyes too.

"Yip," she said, "you're late."

"So what?" said Yip.

"So, you'll get fired. What on earth do you do these days," she demanded, "sleep in your clothes? You look like a collection for the relief."

Yip grinned. He said, "Gee, Jenny, I was out last night . . . I went to the Barnacle and had me a time."

The Barnacle was one of the new juke-box places. It was out near Dorrit's Wharf, on the bay.

Jenny said, "What you kids see in those places . . . !"

"Fun and games," explained Yip, and yawned. "Jive. We cut a rug. We're hep."

Jenny said, "I like swing but I've always thought the language a little disconcerting. Where do you get the gas?"

He said vaguely, "Oh, some of the kids' fathers have C cards, and we can hitchhike or ride a bike out. It's sharp, Jenny. It's the best place, I think, though the Nook isn't too bad. They've a mammoth juke box . . . The girls like it — you can always get a date to go to the Barnacle or the Nook."

"The girls," said Jenny, "what do they do, lie on the floor and squeal at a Sinatra number?"

"Not my girls," said Yip. "I'd wring their necks if they went limp on me over the

Voice. Jenny, you going to the Country Club dance?"

She said, "Yes, the Richards have asked Ede and me."

Mr. Richards had been her boss in personnel. The families were old friends. Jenny's father had been one of the founders of the club. He had deeded the club the land on which it stood. Gram had resigned, for the family, years ago but the directors had paid no attention. The Newtons were given life memberships and paid no dues. For that reason Jenny went seldom to the club. But everyone went to the Decoration Day dance, the Fourth of July and Labor Day parties. And Ede was dying to go. She hadn't danced in a long time. She loved it, she was a beautiful dancer. And Jenny had a new frock. She had saved for it, and it was an extravagance. The buyer at the Seahaven Dress Corner had bought it for her in Boston. Jenny refused to admit to herself that she had bought it because she thought that, possibly, Justice and his sister might be there. She added, and his sister, because it sounded better, in her mental ears. Not that she knew Mary Hathaway. She saw her only when she came to the office, usually to cash a check. But Mary was always extremely nice to her, probably because of Ede. With spring here, Ede was at the

Hathaways' quite a good deal.

She said, "Yip, will you get to work?"

Yip would go to the dance, with the younger crowd. That was the pleasant thing about Seahaven. You walked down the street and you had been to school with the butcher, the baker, the candlestick maker, likewise the banker, the broker, the lawyer and the clergy. Everyone went to the same school, at different times, according to their ages. Some left and went on to prep and then college. Some went to college straight from High. Others, to the Point or Annapolis. And some, right to work.

Yip wouldn't have a junior membership, his mother couldn't afford that, or one for herself. But his best friend was the son of the town's leading banker, Mr. Harris. He'd go with Pooch Harris.

Wonderful nicknames.

She was smiling when someone touched her shoulder. She turned and her heart jumped. Justice. He asked, "Daydreaming on my time? What in the world is clattering around in my office? Mice with GI boots?"

She said, "Yip. He's late. Don't frown and howl at him or he'll burst a blood vessel. He and his gang were rollicking — is there such a word? — at a juke-box joint last night. He's late, and sleepy. It won't happen again

66

. . . I hope." She added, "At least, these places, though they must be noisy to the point of insanity, are harmless . . . cokes, music, youthful jollity."

He said, "You sound elderly this morning."

Jenny said, "I feel quite young . . . about thirty-five. There's a letter from England, on your desk."

"Good," he said, but did not hasten to open and read it, which pleased her, though it should not have done so. Justice wrote his wife twice a week. He dictated the letters to Jenny. Privately, Jenny thought them very dull. If she were Mrs. H. and received such mail, she'd stay in England for the duration. Or maybe, thought Jenny, if she hadn't stayed as long as she had already, she wouldn't have such letters. A very vicious circle. If Justice added something personal, it was after signing. Sometimes he'd scrawl a line or two, shove it in the envelope, and seal it.

He went into his office and Jenny's telephone rang. She answered it and Mary Hathaway's voice came over the wire, like poured cream. She asked, "Jenny? My dear, would you remind Justice that we want a table at the club for the Decoration Day dance?"

Jenny said she would.

When she answered Justice's buzzer a moment later she dutifully reminded him. He scowled at her. He looked very Rochester — Brontë, not Benny — when he scowled. He said, "Hell!"

Jenny grinned. "On you it looks good," she commented.

"What does?"

"That frown."

Justice smoothed his forehead with a mental iron. He said, "I apologize. This club business is a bore. My father's coming up, and probably some New York people. Make it for — let's see — eight . . . On the porch, if it's warm."

The Hathaways joined everything. They were civic. They went to Town Meetings, they were members of the club, they served on various boards. They contributed to all local benevolences, helped build library wings, buy high school projectors, bird sanctuary land.

It is darned funny, Jenny thought, that they haven't been taken in. She was a little impatient with it. It was her first personal experience of Seahaven's tight, traditional reserve. When she spoke of it to her grandmother, Emily Newton merely remarked that you couldn't teach an old dog new tricks.

Absurd, with the world standing on end!

Jenny said, "All right, I'll telephone at once. You won't be too bored. You know everybody and the first dance is fun, usually. Me, I can't wait."

He said, "You're going."

It was not a question but a statement and it puzzled her. Had it been a question, it might have annoyed her and she would have retorted, in her mind, Sure, even the hired help goes, darling! But the statement seemed odd.

She said, "Usually, we do . . ."

He was silent, fussing with the papers on his desk, picking up the airmail letter from England, holding it absently in his hand. He said, "I recall that someone — my sister, I think — said that the property has been in your family — Your father was president, wasn't he, until his death?"

"That's right," said Jenny.

She supposed that being president of a small-town country club didn't rate, with Justice. But if your father, or ancestor, had been president of the Harvard, the Union League, the Racquet — Jenny got around, she read papers and slick magazines — or — she chuckled, the Stork Club . . .

"What are you laughing at?" asked Justice.

"Myself," said Jenny, "I think I'm a frustrated comic."

Justice laughed too. He said, "You are the least frustrated human being I've ever seen. Refreshing, in a way."

She reminded herself that Charlotte had said that Mr. Hathaway might find his new secretary refreshing.

He added, "It must be nice to be young."

Jenny asked politely, "You have probably forgotten?"

He was about thirty-five. He looked up quickly and saw her eyes. He said, "Jenny, in the words of Yip, you slay me." Yip was still fussing around, doing multiple small good deeds. At the sound of his name, he vanished, hair on end.

"Good God," said Justice, "that's the damnedest kid!"

"He's just young, too," said Jenny.

She left the room a moment later to dial the country club number and after that to put in a long distance call. Justice looked after her. Funny youngster. He liked her, but she made him feel uneasy. Her extreme youth, perhaps — which had nothing to do with her age, for he had known a number of twenty-year-old girls who were not young at all — her naturalness, easy, unaffected, her lack of sex appeal. No. She had plenty, he thought, but didn't use it. It was a weapon she had not yet discovered. When she did, there could be fireworks. The thought interested him. He contemplated it. He considered its possibilities and rejected them. Too many complications. But if she were like her sister —

She wasn't.

He thought, Jenny is as competent as Charlotte, in a much less obvious way, and she is not disturbing to have around. The Charlotte situation had been unfortunate. A man drifts into such a corner. A pretty woman, who is not too openly on the make. Overtime, in a quiet Manhattan office, sandwiches sent in and the next time, "Let's get out of here and have dinner somewhere. You look tired. How about soothing music and a very dry Martini?"

Naturally Charlotte had come with him to Seahaven. The affair had been in its most exciting stage then. She had had a flat in the quiet part of town . . . in the only really modern apartment building, and no questions asked. Andrea had gone to England.

Fun and games, and then a burden. Light and gossamer as cobwebs at first but cobwebs have unexpected strength . . . they cling . . . you thought you'd destroyed them and then you found bits brushing across your face, eerie and distasteful.

He had never told Charlotte he would ask Andrea for a divorce. He and Andrea shared nothing. But his father would blow his top if there were a divorce in the family. The Hathaways, in his father's generation, had suffered a number of scandals — a suicide, an embezzlement — but marriage had been Sacred with a capital letter. Justice grinned wryly. His father and mother had deeply disliked each other but they had stuck. He and Mary had grown up wishing to heaven they had come unstuck. It would have been less hard on their children.

But his mother had died, indignantly. She had not expected to die first.

Well, perhaps he *had* told Charlotte there might be a divorce. He hadn't meant it. Few men do, although all promise, or suggest, or pledge in the circumstances. When the heat's on. But even then they hope to heaven that the women to whom they promise, suggest, or pledge are realistic enough to know that there are times that a man will say anything . . . and keep his mental fingers double crossed.

He'd never been in love with Charlotte.

Well, Charlotte was washed out. And he had been ass enough to get himself right into another situation. It was because of that, perhaps, that Charlotte had resigned . . . in more ways than one. Not that she had said anything, but she must have had an inkling. She knew the answers, he had taught them to her to a certain extent.

He thought, *If the boy had lived.*

If Andrea had been a normal woman . . . by God, she wasn't normal, she couldn't be — or she would have recovered from the blow eventually and returned to being his wife. Oh, she would have always been unhappy about it, for when the child was born she had been told that she could never bear another. She would have mourned always, as any woman would. But not in this way.

Chapter Six

The Richards came to take Jenny and Ede to the dance at the club. Jenny was in a froth. She drove Gram crazy and she even distracted Butch's attention from her four kittens. Butch kept bringing them into the room . . . any room, wherever anyone was, and laying them at people's feet. Butch would ask, in her teakettle voice, "Have you ever seen anything so superb? . . . and the image of their dear father!"

Handsome of Butch, thought Jenny, who was the interpreter of her cat's complacent purring, as she had known the infants' father but briefly. And probably didn't even know his name. "Butch," Jenny would ask, "have you seen Pop lately?" and Gram would say, with a subdued twinkle, "Jenny, you are indecent."

Jenny's new dress was white. It was soft, charming, and widely sashed in blue. She said, "I look like Elsie Dinsmore, and it's fun, because at heart I'm Scarlett O'Hara." So misleading. Her hair was a burnished beacon and she had discovered a devastating new shade of lipstick.

Ede selected black, a trousseau frock which she had scarcely worn. It was a print, delicately patterned in pale green, with a tiny jacket. She had bought it in the shop where she had modeled, at, of course, a discount, but even so, it had been expensive. But it was wonderful on her.

The Richards were very nice people, comfortable to be with . . . and you didn't have to make conversation. Jenny was glad driving out to the club. She thought, *He'll ask me to dance.*

They turned into the club driveway, lights came streaming out to meet them, and they could hear music and beyond it the sound of water breaking against the rocks and then rushing smoothly up to hiss on the wet brown sand. They heard music and saw, as Mr. Richards let them out at the steps and went off to park the car, the people moving in the big rooms and on the porch. They heard laughter and smelled cigarette smoke and the war seemed far away.

And Ede thought, I've never been to the Country Club with Dick. He doesn't even know what it looks like. Or did we drive out here once and look at it, when it was closed and shuttered? She couldn't remember. But this place was not associated with her husband, it was associated with the life she had lived before she met him. Going up the steps, meeting people she had always known, drawing Jenny with her into the powder room, she felt that she was once more Edith Newton and not Edith Ainslee. She felt as if she had always been Edith Newton, as if her brief life with Dick were a dream once dreamed. She stared at herself in the mirror and Jenny said impatiently, "Hurry up, Ede, for heaven's sake, you can't do a thing to your face, it's all right as it is!"

Ede rose from before the mirror. Her creamy skin was slightly flushed, her full mouth heavily rouged. Her hair looked as if it had been washed in pure gold. She smiled, her long eyes bright.

Jenny said, "Hurry, dope! I'm starved. It will be a toss-up whether I just sit and eat, or whether I dance . . . providing anyone asks me."

Justice would ask her; he couldn't come in and see her, and not, she thought — or could he?

The Richards had a table for four on the porch. Next to it was a big table, not yet occupied. Jenny's pulse quickened. Bet that's the Hathaways, she told herself. She poked Ede. She said, "The Hathaways will probably be next to us . . . I ordered a table for eight — and that's eight — and it's the only one left."

Ede asked, "Well, what of it?"

Oh, heck, thought Jenny, subdued, naturally she isn't all hot and bothered over a dance at the club. Dick's not here . . . heaven alone knows where he is. You can't expect her to get very excited about tonight.

She thought, sitting down, If Steve were here it would be like old times — almost.

There were many uniforms in the room, men from the nearest camps and naval bases, and men home on leave. The Richards were amused. Jenny had little time in which to eat the routine food of club dinners. One bite, and then, "May I?" and off she went. She knew most of the men here on leave, and many stationed near Seahaven recently. Ede knew them too . . .

The Hathaways arrived late enough to make an entrance. Jenny had just concluded a strenuous turn with the Navy when they arrived. She saw them come in — evidently all the New York guests had not materialized because there were only four in the party, Justice, Mary, their father, a heavy, distinguished-looking man, and another, a younger man whom Jenny did not know. Mary saw them and waved, and a moment later Justice came to their table, smiled at

Jenny and Ede and addressed himself to Richards. He asked pleasantly:

"Won't you join us? We're rattling around at our table. At the last minute three of our expected house guests could not come . . . we'd be most grateful . . . my father has just complained of the lack of feminine company."

The Richards accepted, Richards with a sigh of resignation. After all, he saw enough of the Hathaways at the yard. Mrs. Richards, however, was eaten with curiosity. She had never met the Hathaway men and her acquaintance with Mary was confined to the Red Cross workroom.

They made the change to the larger table and the lone guest was presented. His name was Howard Morgan, he was perhaps forty, and consciously attractive . . . Ede squeezed Jenny's arm. She said, in a whisper, "Mary spoke about him to me. New York, scads of money, divorced, and very attentive to her."

Jenny regarded Mr. Morgan critically. She responded, "He should wear a sign reading 'Danger — wolf at work.' "

The waiter shuffled chairs, brought plates. The fruit cup and soup courses were over for the Richards party, and the Hathaway party waived it. They would start together on the inevitable chicken, mashed potatoes and green peas. But Justice rose again, almost at once, and asked Ede to dance. They moved off across the floor and Jenny looked after her sister with envy. But her turn would come later. And she couldn't blame any man for making her second choice.

Mary Hathaway was watching too. She had just refused to dance with Mr. Morgan. She commented to Jenny, "How well they dance together."

Mary was a good-looking young woman. She was just thirty. Her black hair was as polished as jet, her dark eyes tilted at the corners, and her skin was as good as nature had made, and cosmetics preserved it. She had a smiling, small mouth which always looked amused at something secret. Her figure was exceptionally good, and her charm was as much personality as appearance and clothes. She wore red. It was not a color most women select in the late spring season. It was too warm, too gay. Late May called for pastels or white or the sharp contrast of black. But Mary wore red as if she were wrapped in flame. Yet she somehow contrived to look cool, as if no fire could ever warm her.

Mr. Morgan, his eyes on Mary, sighed and politely requested Jenny to dance. She did so, dutifully suiting her light step to his rather heavy going. He made conversation and she listened. She watched Ede and Justice when she could, they were dancing, not talking. At the table Mary was sitting smoking, looking beautiful and bored and old Mr. Hathaway was talking to the Richards.

The music halted and the dancers returned to their tables. A little later Jenny, dutifully answering questions from the senior Mr. Hathaway who had developed an interest in the early days of the yard, and who had, through the Richards, managed to connect Jenny with the earlier Newtons, looked at her salad and decided that whoever had invented the combination of limp pineapple, macerated lettuce and cream cheese should be shot at dawn. But when the music began again, and Justice asked, "How about it?" she literally flew from the table and into his arms. He asked, smiling, "You like to dance?"

"I love it," she said.

She was silent and happy, dancing with him. It was the first time she had been close to him, the first time her awareness of him was so sharp, definite and exciting. It was not to be the last, but it was the only time she was to take pleasure in it.

When they all returned to the table Mary, who had been dancing with Morgan — and evidently quarreling with him, from his expression — looked across the room and asked, "Who in the world is that, just coming in?"

Everyone looked up at the young man standing in the doorway. He wore civilian clothes. He stood quietly, watching, his right hand in his pocket. He had thick fair hair, and intent eyes, and there were deep lines around his mouth. He was a tall man, a little too thin. His face was fine and stubborn, and remote.

Apparently no one else had seen him until then. Jenny went scarlet with excitement. She cried, *"Ede . . . it's Steve!"* and rose and was halfway across the room before anyone could stir. And Mary, looking at Ede, inquired, "Steve?"

"Steve Barton, the doctor's son," said Ede. "He's a doctor too, just invalided out of the Navy. But we didn't know he was coming today."

She rose, and Mary said quickly, "Bring him back to the table, unless he's looking for someone special."

"I fancy," said Ede, "he was looking for Jenny."

Mary's dark shining eyebrows lifted, for a moment.

The Richards excused themselves and went toward the door. Other people had left their tables and a little reception for Dr. Barton was in progress, but Jenny had arrived first, she was holding his left hand in hers, crying, "But how — when — why didn't you tell us?"

Steve said, in his deep voice, "I hitchhiked a ride . . . by air. I didn't know ahead, myself . . . I phoned Dad this evening from the airport so that I wouldn't take him too much by surprise. I called you, Jenny, after I got in and heard you were out of town . . . so I came to —"

But he had to turn, to be kissed by elderly women, pounded on the back by old men and young. He had to say, over and over, "Sure, I'm fine," and "Yes, I'm home for good."

Ede spoke to him. She said, "Steve, when the reception's over, will you come to our table? The Hathaways . . . a royal command," she added, smiling.

"Hathaways?" He grinned. "Oh, the Boss," he said, with mock reverence, to Jenny. "Okay, for a little while . . . I'm going to pick up Dad later."

He went back to the table with them, finally, Richards on one side and Jenny on the other. The presentations were made. The senior Hathaway was very stuffed shirt, Jenny thought. He made quite a speech. He knew Steve's father, he said, a fine man, a credit to the town. He welcomed Steve home again. He talked like a couple of mayors.

But Mary didn't. She widened her brown eyes and produced an enchanting smile. She managed things so that Steve sat beside her. She said, with disarming frankness, "Well, thank God you're home. It's time that Seahaven offered some — excitement."

"I," said Steve Barton, "am an entirely negative person."

"Meaning," said Mary, "that you always say no?"

She smiled again. Looking up, seeing him there had been the first interesting thing that had happened to her for a long time. She couldn't analyze it. He was not particularly unusual in appearance. Yet there was something hard and aloof about him which attracted and challenged her imagination.

Jenny had seen that, too. He has changed, she thought unhappily. Naturally, he would, after his experiences, and yet she had not expected that he would — toward her. She flushed, remembering how she had whiffed across the room and flung herself at him. His greeting had been amused, but hardly impassioned. She could not understand it. She and Steve . . . pepper and salt, ham and eggs, brandy and soda, anything that went together. She felt as if she were back in her gangling days, pursuing a kindly but bored and impatient young man who looked upon her as an irritating younger sister.

He looked at her now across the table. He said, "Jenny, you've grown up."

Mary asked, "Did you expect her to remain eighteen or whatever she was? After all, she's being exposed to an intensive course in — maturity." She looked fleetly at her brother, who was talking to Ede. Justice sat next to Jenny but he had turned a little away from her.

Jenny's chin went up. She didn't like that remark, nor the tone, nor the thoughtful regard Steve accorded her. Mary said, "Tell us something about your experiences or would you rather not, Dr. Barton?"

He smiled at her amiably. He said, "I'd much rather not. Suppose you tell me about yours?"

Mr. Hathaway cut in. He said, "Mary, you are forgetting your duties as hostess. Have you dined, doctor — and won't you, if you haven't? How about a drink?"

Steve said, "I've dined, thanks, but I could do with a drink."

Almost everyone, the Richards, Mr. Hathaway, Mary and even Howard Morgan were concentrating on Steve. Jenny felt as

84

flat as last night's champagne. She felt out of it. There was the beginning of a pout in her mind. This was quite different from what she had expected when she had learned that Steve would soon be coming home.

There was something sharper about him, the quick laughter had gone, the warmth she had known and counted on, all her days. He was very nearly a stranger, this young man, sitting there, hiding his right hand. He couldn't hide it all the time. He reached for the glass they brought him and she saw the stiff fingers, the drawn flesh, the scar running up the wrist, hidden, eventually, by his cuff.

Mary looked too. She spoke and Jenny heard her. She asked carelessly, "You aren't going to let *that* throw you?"

It was the right thing to say apparently, no sympathy, just a question that was almost a statement. Steve smiled, lopsidedly. He answered, "No, I suppose not."

Jenny drank some black coffee. She heard Justice say to Ede, "The returned hero seems to have made an impression upon my exacting sister," and heard Ede laugh. Then she heard something else. Justice lowered his voice but there was a little cone of silence around Jenny at the moment. The others talked and laughed together, and Justice and

Ede conducted their personal conversation. She was alone, and she could hear . . .

Ede asked, "Do you never think of Boston, Justice, and the wind across the Common and how cold it was, and how afterwards we — ?"

He said sharply, "I told you it was one of the things we'd forget. A mistake on both sides. Too dangerous. Too — unrewarding."

It wasn't much. It was enough. They had been in Boston together. They had . . .

Jenny's throat tightened. She thought she must weep or scream. She thought she must rise and leave this room, get away, by herself, try to think this out. But what was there to think? More important, what was there to *know?*

They might have met by accident, walking on the Common in the sharp wind. They might have — afterward — oh, gone somewhere, for a cup of tea, a cocktail. Harmless enough. They knew each other slightly. When you encounter people you know slightly, suddenly and in another setting, you always believe you know them better than you do. You cry, "Well, for heaven's sake!" You say, "Let's go and have a drink or something."

But Ede had never mentioned it. Ede hadn't been in Boston.

Jenny's hands grew cold. Ede had gone away — in April, wasn't it? — to visit a friend in Worcester, for a weekend. She had come back, full of stories about Edna and her pretty home and her twins.

She could have gone to Edna's, and then to Boston.

Jenny's heart grew as cold as her hands. She remembered the girl on the bus, Agnes Simpson, who said she hadn't seen Ede for a month, at a time when Ede had reported spending an afternoon with her. She remembered the parked car at the empty lot. She remembered Charlotte saying she had seen Justice and Ede in Boston and then correcting herself quickly — it might have been someone who looked like Ede, she'd amended. She remembered Justice asking about Ede, very casually.

How far had it gone? How much did it mean, to Ede? That it meant anything to Justice, Jenny could not believe. She forced herself to look at him. He was still the same, almost indecently attractive. But all she had felt for him, the half-laughing, half-grave, wholly exciting appeal he had had for her, was gone. That hadn't meant anything either, she told herself stubbornly, but it had been — oh, fun, an accelerated heartbeat, and something to look forward to when you rose in the morning and set about the business of getting ready to go to work.

Ede, she thought passionately, *how could you?*

Ede was married. She was married to a man who was overseas fighting, sweating it out in dripping jungles, sleeping with fear, waking to it . . . tortured by heat and insects, facing, by day, by night, an implacable, almost subhuman enemy. Dick Ainslee was a real person. He was a fine man. He was terribly in love with his wife. He merited her love, her fidelity.

There was a sudden commotion over toward the bar door, which created a diversion. Even Steve and Mary looked up from their smiling absorption in one another. Steve, his drink warming and relaxing him, was having a pretty good time. He was home. And he was with strangers. That was better. You eased into things that way. Too many friends, commiserating, that was bad, and very hard. Jenny, for instance, her child's face flushed with happiness, her eyes radiant. Just a kid . . . He'd always been fond of her. But he didn't want people he was fond of, at the moment. Except, of course, his father. And his father's condition lay like a burden upon his mind and heart. It quickened him with anger and rebellion.

Not for himself . . . but for the older man. Why did that have to happen to a man like Bert Barton, a whole and useful man?

As for himself, his duty lay clear. It was distasteful, it wasn't what he had planned nor wanted, but there it was. He owed it to his father. And he had thought, grimly, earlier in the evening, and no back talk to myself about sacrifices. I'm sacrificing nothing. My hand sees to that. What else could I do even if Dad were himself?

Mary asked, "What in the world is going on?"

He liked Mary. He had not met her before although he had seen her briefly on several occasions before he went away. He hadn't seen a woman like her since . . . You didn't see women like Mary where he'd been. She was all the things — well, some of them — that you thought about, out there . . . she wasn't the friendly, warm, close things that meant home, the mothering things, the consoling. She was the other side of the picture, entertainment, lightness, and that much overworked word "glamour." A little hard, as he himself had become hard. That was all right too. Sex and mentality in a pretty package.

Richards had left the table and gone toward the scene of the disturbance, and after a moment Steve excused himself and fol-

89

lowed. When they returned Richards was very grave but Steve was grinning, slightly. He said, in answer to Mary's raised eyebrows, "Just kids — they've been celebrating."

"That's hardly the way to look at it," said Richards sharply. "That was Yip Morrison whom you know very well and Pooch Harris and a couple of girls whom I don't know. And they were all *drunk.*"

He had raised his voice. Mrs. Richards cried, shocked, "But where — ? How — ? They're under age, it wouldn't be sold to them here . . . or anywhere."

Richards sat down. He said, "Luckily Harris was in the other room. He's taken them home. From what I gathered, they were trying to buy another drink at the bar. And they won't say where they got what they've already had. I suppose they swiped it, at home, took it out in a car . . . sounds like the twenties all over. But it's a problem." He looked at Jenny and shook his head. He said, "I'll have a talk with Yip. If — if this happens again, we'll have to let him go."

Jenny said, "I don't believe he got anything at home. There's just his mother. I doubt if she has liquor in the house."

Richards said, "I've been wondering for some time if these juke-box places sell anything on the sly, to minors. I've heard complaints before . . . oh, nothing specific, but just that the kids are drinking. It's time someone looked into it."

Mr. Hathaway said soothingly, "Perhaps we are making a mountain out of a molehill. It's quite possible, as you said, that one of the youngsters stole a bottle at home —"

Jenny looked at Steve. She thought, He knows Yip, he knows all the kids. Why isn't he more excited about it? But Steve was talking to Mary.

She thought, It's as if he didn't care any more what happens here.

"Justice," said Ede, low, urgently.

Jenny heard that too. She thought, I'll be damned if I'll let her! She thought, I'm not married. I work with him every day. I can make him know I'm alive, if I want to . . . I haven't — I liked it just as it was . . . fun, and no heartaches. I'll turn those pictures to the wall and I'll —

Not that I want him, she thought, but *there's Dick.*

She touched Justice's arm, and when he turned she said, "It's all very well to concentrate on Ede, but I'm feeling neglected. The music's started . . ."

He said, astonished and amused, "I'm at your service, Jenny."

Dancing, she moved closer to him than she had before and he was again astonished, and quite entertained. Jenny danced as well as her sister. And he was tired of her sister; tired of chains, of tears and self-reproaches and all the old why-did-this-have-to-happen business. Edith Ainslee wasn't in love with him, she was still in love with her husband, she was simply bored and lonely . . . and so was he. He had wanted to keep it on that plane. But one never could.

The girl in his arms was neither bored nor lonely. Her red hair glittered in the light, and she danced with her luminous blue eyes half closed and a small, quiet smile on her pretty mouth. She wasn't reproachful, she had no tears to shed, unless they were warm tears, sudden as May rain, and as quickly dried.

He said, "You know, Jenny, you're quite a girl."

"It's about time you discovered it," said Jenny, opened her eyes, and smiled. "You're awfully slow on the uptake, Justice."

Steve was watching them, his brows tight. The man held Jenny too close and she seemed to like it. She was being, he thought, a little obvious. And Mary asked, "Why the scowl, Dr. Barton?"

He said, "Sorry. I was watching my young

friend Jenny. It seems to me, she has grown up in a hurry."

"You mean, of course, my brother," said Mary lazily. "I told you she had been exposed to maturity. Justice is quite a menace . . ."

Steve said shortly, "I thought he was married."

Mary shrugged. She asked, "What kind of marriage is it which keeps a wife away from her husband for four years, fighting a war? Quite a reversal of the usual routine, isn't it? Besides, Andrea, while beautiful, is a saint and it isn't easy to live with saints, even when they descend from their private heaven."

Mary knew about Ede . . . It hadn't bothered her. She was tolerant to the point of laxity. She liked Ede, she was sorry for her, and if Ede and Justice elected to amuse themselves, it wasn't her business. But tonight the picture had changed. She had met Steve Barton, of whom Ede had said carelessly, "I dare say he's looking for Jenny."

If he were looking for Jenny with serious intentions, if he had been looking for, and at, her for years, it was time his attention was distracted. She said lightly, "All my brother's secretaries fall in love with him."

"And who," he asked gravely, "falls in love

with you, Miss Hathaway?"

She said, "That depends upon whom I wish —" She broke off. She added, "I feel a slight leprosy coming on, doctor."

"Which suits me," he responded, "perfectly."

His heart was thick with anger. He had always thought that when Jenny grew up she would be worthy of any man's attention. He hadn't expected to find her making herself unworthy — and cheap.

He rose presently. It was time for him to call for his father; he made his apologies and thanks. He nodded at Jenny and Ede. "I'll be over sometime tomorrow," he said and went out. People stopped him, and some followed him. But he shook them off, courteously, and went on out, a somehow lonely figure.

Mary drew a deep breath. She said deliberately, to Howard Morgan's annoyance, "Well, life in Seahaven is beginning to look up. I don't think that, after all, I'll go away this summer."

Chapter Seven

The Richards took Ede and Jenny home. It was late and Jenny had danced almost every dance with Justice. He had been a willing partner. Far better that he dance with Jenny than with Ede. He wanted no more of that. They had washed it up the other night, when they'd gone for a drive and, later, parked. That is, he thought they had; apparently Ede hadn't.

Ede and Jenny went into the house in silence, and up the stairs. Gram was a very light sleeper. When they reached Jenny's door, Ede said, "Good night, Jen . . ."

She didn't want to talk about the evening nor even about Steve and his sudden interest in Mary Hathaway, nor Mary's in him. That could wait and it wasn't important to her, at the moment, whether it was to Jenny or not. Nor could she demand of Jenny, What was the meaning of your extraordinary behavior tonight? An older sister could, in other circumstances, even to the reading of the riot act. But not Ede. She was too vulnerable. She might betray herself.

But Jenny caught her hand and drew her into her room and shut the door. She stood there, small, and erect, and her eyes blazed with anger. She said, "Just a moment. I overheard something tonight which made me put two and two together and get a sum I don't like. You've been seeing Justice Hathaway, for, I think, quite a long time. Have you had, are you having an affair with him?"

Ede's face altered. For just a split second before expression returned, it became blank, almost stupid with shock. Then her eyes and mouth came alive again, her color rose hotly, and her regard was hostile, defiant. Yet during that swift change she had looked old — and apprehensive. Jenny's heart tightened intolerably.

Edith asked coolly, "Are you out of your mind?"

Jenny felt as if she would fly to pieces, she wanted to stamp her foot, childishly. She wanted to cry. She said, instead, as coolly:

"Don't give me that routine. It's just stalling. I am not out of my mind but I think you are. I've been pretty dumb, Ede. I didn't think you even knew Justice Hathaway except by sight — I'd even forgotten you'd met him through his sister at their house. And then Charlotte Granley said she'd seen you together in Boston."

Ede said angrily, "That's the sort of thing she *would* say . . ." She caught herself, and stopped, but not quite in time.

"Why?" asked Jenny. "You don't know *her*. So you must have heard about her . . . and there's no one who'd tell you about her except — her ex-boss."

Ede said sullenly, "There's Mary . . ."

"I doubt if she'd discuss Charlotte Granley with you," Jenny retorted. "But it wasn't just Charlotte. It was Agnes Simpson, meeting me on the bus and saying she hadn't seen you for weeks, right after you'd told Gram and me you'd spent the afternoon with her. It was seeing you, with my own eyes, in the Hathaway car, and especially overhearing what you said to Justice, tonight . . ."

Ede grew white. The anger which had informed her, burned out. In its place there was an enormous weariness, blurring her beauty. She asked flatly, "What did you hear?"

"You asked him," said Jenny, "if he ever thought of Boston, and walking across the Common and now cold it was and —"

Ede said wildly, "All right, then. Have it your own way. I have been seeing him, off and on. As for Boston, it was an accident. I went to Worcester, Edna had to go to Boston so I trailed along . . . I ran into Justice and we had a drink at the Ritz and then I met Edna and went on back with her —"

It was very thin. It was like gauze. You saw through it. Yet, it was possible, perfectly possible. Jenny said, with sudden, aching sorrow, "I do so want to believe you, Ede."

Ede sat down on Jenny's bed. She put her hands over her face, the long, luxury-loving hands with their painted nails. Her hair was a golden glow about her abased head. She said, muffled, "You'll never understand."

Jenny knelt by the bed. Her heart was beating in slow, sickening pulsations. She said, "I'll try, Ede, I promise."

Ede took her hands away and stared straight ahead of her. She said, after a moment:

"I'm in love with Dick. I'm terribly in love with him. I keep telling myself that, all the time. Especially when I'm alone, shut up in my old room here, at night. Lying awake. Thinking about him, thinking about us, and wondering. Trying to remember what he looks like. You don't know what a special sort of hell that is, Jenny. To try to remember how the person you love looks — and how his voice sounds. You can remember the words he said but you can't remember his voice."

She broke off. Then she went on, her voice low and harsh, her brown eyes dry, and a little distended:

"I'm lonely, I — I've been married. Before I was married I had a good time. Even here at home. Excitement," she said, "attention. Then, after I went away, I was on my own . . . It was gay, it was amusing. Always someone to take you out to dinner, or buy you a cocktail and tell you that you were pretty, that you were exciting . . ." She moved her shoulders restlessly. "I could have . . ." She halted again. She said, "I didn't. Funny, but the men who, if you're on your own, pay you the most attention, they're married, as a rule. The younger ones, those who aren't married, well, those I met couldn't afford orchestra seats and flowers and all the rest. But I was just being awfully entertained, Jenny. I didn't fall in love or even think I could until I met Dick —"

Jenny was silent, kneeling there. She was aware of a feeling of complete dissociation. This sort of thing happened to other people, it happened in books and plays, but not to her and Ede. A scene like this, packed with violence and anger and hurt. The things she'd said, the things Ede had said — and left unsaid. It wasn't real. Yet the room was real and familiar, and the one light shining.

The house was real, the house in which she had lived for twenty years. She could hear the soft teakettle purring from the basket on the other side of the room in which Butch lay, with her kittens. She could feel Gram in the house, quiet in the light sleep of old age, not far away. She could smell the spring through the opened windows.

Ede said, "You aren't listening. Jen, listen to me! I didn't want this to happen. I saw Justice Hathaway first when I went to Mary's . . . No, that's not true. I let him pick me up one day, I'd been shopping, I stopped at the Tavern and had a cup of tea, and he was there, in the bar, and he came over. He knew me. He said, 'I've heard about you from Mary . . .' "

Jenny did not speak. Ede went on, presently: "It doesn't matter, does it? How or when or where? I did see him at Mary's. And we had lunch, a day or so later, out of town . . . and it went on like that. I —"

Jenny asked, "Are you in love with him?"

"Oh," said Ede restlessly, "how do I know? Can you love two men at the same time? I keep telling myself, it's Dick, always . . . it's Dick I love and want . . . and miss so dreadfully . . . And keep losing, somehow. Our time was so short," she said passionately. "Can't you understand that? And because I want him and miss him I — There's no use," she told Jenny, and her tone was despairing, "you can't possibly know what it's like. No, I don't love Justice," she concluded, "but he — somehow — he makes me know I'm alive."

Jenny rose. She felt stiff, her knees and her hands and her lips. She moved her lips cautiously and spoke and her voice sounded stiff, too, in her ears.

She said relentlessly, "That's no excuse."

Ede rose too. She said, "You wouldn't know."

Jenny is very young, thought Ede. She can look at me with those accusing eyes but she doesn't understand, she *doesn't*.

"I don't want to know," said Jenny, and she didn't mean what Ede had meant. She didn't want to know whether or not Ede had lied about Boston. She didn't want to know anything. She felt ill. She wanted to say what she had to say and be done with it, for always.

She said, "Millions of other women are waiting, just as you are. A great many of them haven't been married much longer, or as long. Maybe it's hard for them to remember. Yet most of them do." She lifted her red head and looked straight into Ede's somber eyes. "I don't know how far this has gone

101

between you and Justice, I don't want to know. But whether you met on the Common, as you said, by accident or whether you never went to Worcester but straight to Boston to spend the weekend there with him, isn't entirely the point. When I think of Dick, I think of all the men like him, sweating, dying, fighting. It's no good, Ede. Just because you're lonely . . . Do you suppose Dick isn't lonely? You frighten me," she said, "and you — disgust me."

Ede was scarlet. She was hostile again, with anger renewed. She said, "What I do or don't do isn't your business. It's mine!"

"And Dick's?" Jenny inquired.

"All right," said Ede, "Dick's, if you want it that way. But not yours."

"I'll make it my business," Jenny promised. "After Dick gets home you can do as you please. That's between you and him. But until he does . . ." She stopped and then said evenly, "You'll stop seeing Justice Hathaway . . . I'll stop you."

"How?" asked Ede sharply.

Jenny said, "There are ways." She looked at Ede, her eyes brilliant. "I'll find one."

Ede walked to the door. She paused, with her hand on the knob. She asked, quite casually, "I suppose you intend to tell Gram?"

"No," said Jenny, "I don't. She has enough on her plate. She won't know, from me."

"That's white of you," said Ede. "And Dick?"

Jenny blazed, visibly. She said, "One — heel's enough in the family."

"Thanks," said Ede. She added, "If you aren't going to tattle, then — how?"

Jenny smiled a little and Ede stared at her. She said, startled, "I believe you're in love with him yourself. I believe — Well," said Ede, on a long breath, "the picture begins to come clearer. All this wrath and righteousness, it isn't on my account nor the precious family honor, nor because of Dick. It's because you're in love with him," she said again, "and you're jealous. You think you can —"

Jenny got between Ede and the door. She opened the door and stood there, speaking softly in order not to awaken Gram. She said, "Maybe."

Jenny closed the door, with Ede on the outside of it. She walked blindly toward the bed and sat down. She was shaking, her hands were ice-cold. How much was true, how much was false? She clenched her teeth to keep them from a senseless chattering. She thought, with cold clarity, I can . . . and

I will. I can't be hurt because I'm not really in love with Justice Hathaway . . . It makes me a little sick to think of him. But he won't know that; nor Ede.

She put her head down on her pillows and began to cry. Butch heard her and came soft-stepping, anxiously, to the bed, sprang up and spoke in her velvet cat-voice. And Jenny reached out, clutched her and cried into the soft, silky fur. Butch, a fastidious creature, stirred and pulled herself away. But she did not go back to her basket and her sleeping, captivating kittens. She sat beside Jenny, kneading her paws into Jenny's bare arm, careful not to scratch . . .

After a long time, Jenny rose, and carried Butch to her basket. She took off the new frock, the full white skirt crushed and rumpled, the blue sash creased, and hung it up. She undressed and went to the bathroom and washed. She held a washcloth to her swollen eyes and tried to steady the catch in her breath. She thought, *No matter what happens . . .*

There was no one to whom she could talk except Steve . . . Yet Steve had changed. He wasn't as she had known him, all those years. And even if he had been, she couldn't talk to him, after all, this was something she must keep to herself, and something she had to

do alone. What had Ede said a while ago
. . . "I was on my own." Well, thought
Jenny, I'm on my own too, now.

Chapter Eight

Jenny woke to hot still sunlight. Her first thought was a drowsy dreaming, an awareness of well-being rather than a mental process . . . a consciousness that this was Sunday and that she needn't hurry, that breakfast would be late and leisurely, and that she and Gram and Ede would go to church . . .

Ede.

She remembered now, the sunlight darkened and her sense of well-being vanished. She sat up in bed and stretched her round young arms above her disheveled red head. She heard Gram's voice and thought, suddenly, how hard it would be to keep things from Gram . . . Gram was as sensitive as a barometer and she would be certain to suspect that things were wrong between her granddaughters.

Jenny got out of bed. She thought, I'm a coward. She didn't want to see Ede, she dreaded seeing her. Nor did she want to go to the office tomorrow morning and wait for a door to open and for Justice to walk in saying, "Hi, Jenny . . ."

Instead, she wanted to lock her door, pull down the shades, go back to bed and sleep and sleep.

Butch spoke. She had left her basket and was stretching, relaxed and beautiful, in the middle of the floor. Butch asked, a little peevishly, "Well, are you going to keep us cooped up here all day?"

Jenny opened the door and let her go out, walking in pride and dignity toward her breakfast.

A little later Jenny, with somewhat less pride and dignity, went downstairs. She wore a blue jumper dress with a thin white blouse and she looked about sixteen. She went into the dining room, her hands cold and her heart braced. But Ede, sitting cozily with Gram at the table, raised a lazy eyebrow and smiled at her. She said, "We thought you were dead to the world."

So it was to be like that, on the surface, as if nothing had happened or could happen. Jenny said, "Sorry — I couldn't seem to wake up."

Ede looked as if she had slept for twelve hours. She wore one of her honeymoon housecoats, cool aquamarine in color. Her hair was brushed and shining and she had powdered her face and rouged her pretty mouth. Gram, in thin gray cotton, was refilling her coffee cup.

"Jenny, Ede's been telling me about the Morrison boy and young Harris. It's disgraceful," said Gram, and put the pot down with a slight thump, "and someone ought to do something about it."

"I imagine that the Harrises have," said Jenny, "and as for Yip — well, if he doesn't get a good going-over from Mr. Richards tomorrow, I'll miss my guess."

Gran said, "Ede suggested that the boys took liquor from their homes. I doubt that very much. Someone is selling it to them." Her eyes snapped. "I wish Bert Barton was well enough to take a hand in this. He'd find out and put a stop to it." She picked up the silver pot again and poured Jenny's coffee. She said, "Ede told me about Steve."

Jenny ate her home-canned peaches. They were ice-cold and just sweet enough. Gram, a watchful eye on the waffle iron, asked, "Did you think he had changed, Jenny?"

"Very much," said Jenny.

"He's older," said Ede carelessly, "and —" she shrugged — "well, you can't quite put your finger on it."

"It's natural," said Gram; "after all, he's had a dreadful experience — one which isn't calculated to leave him just as before. And then, too, he's disappointed . . . his life will be different than he'd planned. But he'll come to see that it's a good life," she said firmly, "and useful. He has too much sense not to realize that. He's too fine a boy."

"He'll learn to like it here," said Ede with a faint smile, "already, last night, he drummed up a little fancy practice . . . Mary Hathaway. She seemed very interested in him, didn't you think so, Jenny?" she asked, her eyes guileless. "And he fell for her, too, hammer and tongs."

"Well," said Jenny, "she's very attractive."

She thought that over, eating Gram's waffles, with the good Vermont syrup. She'd been so preoccupied with other things that she hadn't thought about Mary and Steve. But, yes, Ede was right. They had seemed definitely attracted to each other. She examined that thought, and found, to her surprise, that she didn't like it. Not because of Steve, Steve could have — and had had, for all Jenny knew — a dozen girls and it was no skin off Jenny's little nose. But . . . must it always be the Hathaways? she thought angrily. I wish they'd never set foot in town!

After breakfast was cleared away and the dishes washed, the usual lazy routine began. Bathe, dress, manicure your nails, and go to church. The three of them. Walking the few blocks, in the bright, hot sunlight. You could smell the shaded, hidden beds of valley lilies, and the lilac scent was heavy on the unstirring air.

After church, Ede went calling. At least she said that was what she was going to do. She looked lovely in her printed silk suit and her absurd hat. She left them at the corner, waved her hand, and vanished. And Gram and Jenny proceeded, sedately, homeward, stopped half a dozen times by their neighbors.

Almost everyone in Seahaven, in Jenny's Seahaven, that is, breakfasted late on Sundays, went to church, and then came home and had a two- or even three-o'clock dinner. After which they sat around in a pleasant coma until it was time for a pickup supper.

Every Sunday Mrs. Moran came to the Newtons' to get dinner. And once a week Mrs. Moran came in to do the heavy cleaning. She was an energetic, middle-aged woman who, before her marriage, had worked steadily at the Newtons'. Now she obliged, by the day. Jenny had insisted that Gram have one day of comparative peace and, so, Sundays when the Newtons returned from church the scent of Mrs. Moran's ineffable cooking filled the house. Gram always seemed astonished. She always hurried in crying, "Nellie must have come early."

After which she would divest herself of her church-going garments, put on something comfortable — and go into the kitchen to superintend dinner and listen to Mrs. Moran's gossip. Not that Gram ever called it gossip. She abhorred gossip and never encouraged it. But she liked to hear what was going on.

She heard plenty today, sitting in the rocker by the open windows while Mrs. Moran busied herself with the fricasseed chicken and opined as how the fowl was a little elderly but still tender enough. Mrs. Moran's niece worked for the Harrises and there had been ructions last night, said Mrs. Moran, which brought Lily, startled, bolt upright out of her needed sleep. The Harrises had come back from the Country Club along with that young limb, Pooch. From all Lily could learn Pooch had been drinking. "At his age!" said Mrs. Moran severely, "and where did he get the stuff, anyway? And not only him but the Morrison kid and the girls with them." Not that she knew who the girls were but she pitied their poor mothers.

Jenny went on upstairs. She had a hem to sew, a dozen small Sundays jobs to do. But her needle faltered. She pricked her finger, and the thread broke.

Where was Ede? she thought, looking with

unseeing eyes into the new green of the tree outside her window . . . She couldn't be with Justice . . . This was Sunday. He would be with his father, with Mary . . . and his guests.

Had she really gone calling or had she gone to the drugstore to phone Justice? Was she saying, even now, "Jenny *knows*"?

Jenny hadn't thought of that.

She thought, She has too much pride.

No, she hadn't an atom, or how could she speak as she had at the club . . . begging for his attention, his — interest.

Little Red Ridinghood, Jenny reminded herself, was wolf bait. I won't be. When Ede sees that practically any girl who isn't hard to look at can divert Mr. Wolf . . . she'll cry uncle. She'll stay away from him, in spades.

Jenny thought, She'd better, for if she told the truth, if the Boston incident was an accident, and she didn't spend the weekend with him, well, she just might get ideas. I've made her plenty mad, and she's always been so darned stubborn. And, if it wasn't an accident . . . I've got to prevent its happening again.

Loneliness is no excuse; nor boredom; nor feeling unsure because happiness is brief and waiting long. Maybe the men who fight are uncertain too, of themselves and the girls they love. Maybe they lie awake in the lethal nights and know a closer, more agonizing fear than that of death. The cure is reassurance.

She thought, When people have been married a long time, it's different, trust and certainty are part of their scheme, like breathing. Fidelity is perhaps a habit, of the heart, and mind and body. But kids, thought Jenny, feeling old and grieved, what they have to remember is so easy to forget, after a while.

There was one thing she must believe, and that was that Ede and Dick were essentially right for each other and that when he came home Ede would realize it. Whatever she had done, she must then regret for the rest of her life. But that was up to her. That was the price tag. How high the price, she might not know until she saw Dick again. If when she saw him she no longer wanted him, or if each had outgrown the other, that was something else, and their business. But now Jenny had to go forward on the assumption that one day Dick would come home to a wife who would love and cherish him.

And if he didn't come home?

She shivered and rose, slowly, from her chair. You can't see into the hearts and minds of the people you know and love. How Ede felt, how she would feel whether he came home or not, was hidden from her sister — probably it would always be so. But meantime — no more trips to Boston.

In the afternoon Steve came by. He walked into the hall and inquired in a muted bellow, "Anyone home?"

They were all out on the screened back porch. Mrs. Moran had gone home, Ede was reading the paper and smoking, Gram was knitting, and Jenny just sitting, slumped in a big wicker chair, all angles and knees. Steve, following their answering chorus, came out to join them, caught Gram up, kissed her, and flipped a hand at the girls.

Gram said, after a while, "Steve, tell me honestly what you think of your father's health?"

He looked at her gravely. He was sitting on the end of Ede's long couch, teasing Butch, who appeared to remember him favorably. He answered slowly, "He's pretty sick, Gram."

Her face, fragile as old porcelain, clouded. She said quietly, "I'm grieved to hear that. He's as fine a man as I have ever known, I think. You — well, it's up to you, Steve, to take the burden."

"I will," he told her.

Ede said, "Tell us something about yourself, Steve, and what happened."

He shook his head. "It was — messy," he said, "and disagreeable. I'd rather not think about it. What do you hear from Dick?"

"Not much more than I'm hearing from you," she said. "Letters are unsatisfactory, aren't they?"

"Not letters from home," he told her; "they're a shot in the arm and about the most important thing in a guy's life. The right kind of letters. I've seen men put out of action, literally, by the wrong kind . . . the whining, martyred letter, or the letter with the superfluous bad news . . . they breed an anxiety neurosis. When a guy's killing Japs or Germans, and waiting for the shell or bullet with his name on it, when he's standing on deck or flying a plane, or slogging through the mud or sitting in a machine-gun nest, he's got enough to worry over without worrying about the mortgage or Junior's mumps or the terrible sacrifices of his family," said Steve with bitterness, "in going without gas or beef or Pullman space. I saw one of the toughest Marines in our outfit go to pieces because his mother wrote him a sweet little letter and informed him that she was sure his wife was two-timing him. Good God!"

Ede looked at Jenny, and Jenny felt the

blood rise hot, to her cheeks.

Gram said gently, "You've got to make allowances for human nature, Steve. Much of the world's misery is caused, not by malice, but by selfishness, thoughtlessness and plain downright ignorance."

"That's the sixty-four-dollar answer," said Steve, "but you'd be surprised, Gram, how little even sound philosophy helps when you're too cold or too hot, when your temperature soars and your mind is fuzzy, when you're sick and lonesome and afraid."

Jenny sat bolt upright. This wasn't Steve. This was a man who wore his body, looked from his eyes and spoke with his mouth. Not the Steve who laughed, and wisecracked, and saw the funny side of things; but who was, underneath, eager and understanding, confident of life, excited by it.

Ede spoke quickly. "This is a pretty grim conversation for Sunday afternoon."

Steve turned to look at her. He said, "Sorry, old girl," in a voice Jenny remembered. Her face was composed but her mind made a small grimace. She thought, That's wonderful . . . he's sorry because he believes Ede's thinking about Dick!

Ede said, "That's all right," and pushed aside the papers with the sheets of comics which Jenny read avidly, Ede scorned, and

Gram sneaked up to her room, Sunday nights. Gram was a secret Dick Tracy addict. During the adventures of 88 keys, Prune-Face and Flat-Top, Gram was beside herself in a quiet way. Ede added, changing the subject with calculated deliberation, "Steve, wasn't it too bad about the kids at the club last night?"

He said negligently, "Ought to have their hides tanned. But that's the way things are nowadays, I suppose."

Jenny swung her feet to the floor. "You make me tired, Steve Barton." He regarded her with amused surprise. "A couple of years ago you would have been tearing the town down to find out how it happened. Because it didn't happen at the club, nor at the Harrises, and if Mrs. Morrison owns anything stronger than elderberry wine I'll eat a caduceus. You'd be foaming at the mouth and making inquiries. Uncle Bert will, anyway."

"I didn't tell him," Steve said shortly.

"Someone will," said Jenny, with energy, "and he'll have a fit. He was around when those kids were born. He's always taken an interest in Seahaven youngsters, he's straightened out a lot of 'em, as you know darned well."

He asked mildly, "Do you suggest that I

embark upon a crusade?"

"I don't know about crusades," said Jenny, "but I do think you could get together with Mr. Harris and Mrs. Morrison and see what gives."

"Jenny's right," said Gram.

But Ede laughed. She said, "Pay Jenny no mind, Steve, she's always steamed up about something. And it isn't so world-shattering. Someone gave the kids a drink and they couldn't hold it. It probably won't happen again. I bet they're plenty ashamed today. You only put their backs up when you lecture and threaten."

Well, thought Jenny, that's fine. That's just dandy. She's talking straight at me!

"That's what I think," said Steve.

Jenny ran her fingers through her hair. It stood up like a burning halo.

"You sure have changed," she said.

"Well," asked Steve, with deceptive mildness, "why not? I've been out, dear, out of Seahaven, into the wide wide world. I've come back." He removed his right hand from his pocket and looked at it, absently. "I've a job to do to the best of my ability. I can't say I'm crazy about it. I paid a few calls this morning. No one was very glad to see me. Naturally, they welcomed the hero home, but when they discovered that he

118

meant business with the little black bag and the nasty cold stethoscope, they unwelcomed him. I'm little Steve Barton, the kid who pitched on the team and ran the quarter mile; the kid who used to cut up frogs and bring their daughters home from dances, half an hour late. I'm their doctor's son. So when I said, 'Put out your tongue,' they put it out a good deal farther than was necessary. And asked themselves, 'What the hell does *he* know?' "

Gram started to say, "This is Sunday, Steve," but no one heard her because Jenny was inquiring furiously, "Well, what do you?"

He looked at her and grinned. He said softly, "My, what a long tail our cat has," and Butch pricked up her furry ears. He added, "I'm surprised you haven't started a Good Neighbor club at the shipyard. From all I've heard in the few hours I've been home, you could do with one."

Gram said pacifically, while Ede laughed, "Steve, stop quarreling with Jenny. She's upset and I don't blame her. She's known those boys since they were born and Yip works in the office. Are you staying for supper?"

He said, and Jenny had the feeling that it pleased him to say it, "Sorry, darling, but I'm going to the Hathaways'. They've decided to permit me to break their platinum bread."

Ede cried, "But that's wonderful, Steve. Maybe someone will even break a leg."

"I intend," he replied gravely, "to throw the old man into the swimming pool. Anything for an upper-bracket practice."

Jenny said sweetly, "Why don't you trip Miss Hathaway? I'm sure she'd fall easily."

"Meow," remarked Butch astonishingly, and everyone laughed and the atmosphere cleared.

"Seriously," said Steve, "I promised I'd run over and dunk their doughnuts in vintage champagne. I'll probably get half a dozen calls but Mary assured me it wouldn't matter."

Jenny said, "You have progressed, haven't you?"

He said easily, "These are informal times." He rose and looked down at her. He said, "I like the girl. She has plenty on the ball. She's a change. I haven't been around the pin-up variety lately."

"With the birth rate going up so fast, Steve, you'll see plenty of the pin-up variety," Jenny reminded him.

Steve went over, pulled her up, turned her around and gave her a resounding slap on her pleasant little rear end. She said,

"Ouch," with indignation and he released her. He said, "You've changed, too, my love. And not, I may add, for the better."

He was gone, with that careless flip of his left hand, and Gram said, "I don't think you treated him too well, Jenifer."

"Don't Jenifer me," said Jenny with dignity. "He makes me tired. He doesn't give a hoot what happens to this town. If he lands the Hathaway practice he'll start wearing a gardenia in his buttonhole and cultivating a bedside manner. Mary would like that."

Ede said lazily, "Mary's a friend of mine. Don't you like her?"

"I'm crazy about her," said Jenny, deadpan. "I just dote on the whole family. I think they're wonderful."

Gram sighed. She said, "I wish you'd let me listen to the radio. At least when people bicker over the air I can turn it off . . ."

"Sorry," said Jenny, who wasn't, "but it keeps occurring to me that the South Seas haven't improved Steve. He used to be quite a guy. Now he's just one of those frustrated, embittered men you read about. Why should he be?" she demanded. "He's home, he's alive, and he's got a job to do — and one which will prolong his father's life. He should be grateful on his knees."

"Perhaps," said Gram, "he is, in his heart. Or will be. You're young, Jenny, and your judgments are usually hasty."

"Too hasty," said Ede, "if you ask me."

"I didn't," said Jenny, and departed, Butch at her heels.

Gram looked after them.

"What's got into her?" she demanded.

"Maybe she's in love," suggested Ede; "sometimes it takes people in the oddest ways."

"Steve?" asked Gram. "Well, I always hoped — when she grew up and when he stopped looking on her as a child. But she certainly doesn't act it," she added, bewildered.

"I wasn't thinking of Steve."

"Who else?" Gram asked. "All her old beaux have gone to war. She writes them with praiseworthy regularity but shows me the answers."

Ede said, rustling the paper, "Jenny has a very attractive boss."

Gram sat up, so straight and so suddenly that you could almost hear her spine snap. She said angrily, "Edith Newton Ainslee, that's not a nice thing to say, not nice at all!"

"Why not?" asked Ede. She thought, One up, Jenny.

Gram said, "Mr. Hathaway is a married man."

Ede threw the paper aside. She said, "Gram, stop living in a Victorian dream."

"Men," said Gram, "were married even when Victoria was queen."

"I didn't say anything," said Ede, yawning. "I was just offering a possible explanation. It wouldn't be easy, I dare say, for a girl of Jenny's inexperience to be exposed daily to a man of Justice Hathaway's sunny charm without being — burned."

"If I thought that," said Gram, "I'd insist that she resign her position."

"Just when she's had a raise?" asked Ede. "Don't be impractical, angel. I was thinking about Mr. Hathaway's last secretary. She was a beautiful blonde but she burned, or was burned. She'd been exposed for six years, I understand. It's curious too that Jenny was picked from all the available girls, some with much more experience, after the position became open. Look, Gram. Maybe I'm wrong. Maybe she adores Steve in secret and is just covering up because, to paraphrase the song, he obviously doesn't adore her. You'd only precipitate things if you said anything to her, and there isn't anything to precipitate. Or, if she doesn't know that her boss exists except as a pay check, you'd make her mad as hops or even put the idea into her red head. See?"

"I see," said Gram, "and I don't like what I see."

Chapter Nine

Jenny reluctantly caught her bus next morning. She was not feeling happy. Also, she was scared. What was she supposed to do now? Thump on the desk Yip was supposed to keep dusted and cry, "Mr. Hathaway, I know all. I forbid you to have anything more to do with my sister!"

Nuts, she thought in disgust. Real life wasn't like that. Or was it? Did it run along, as smooth and polite as drawing-room comedy, or an underplayed drama, and then suddenly flare up into naked melodramatics?

If she felt uneasy entering the familiar office, Justice felt much the same when, some time later, he opened the door. Ede had telephoned him. She had said breathlessly, "Justice, I've had the most awful scene with Jenny. It seems that she overheard us talking at the club last night, also she's apparently heard — rumors. Charlotte Granley told her she saw us in Boston. She didn't believe it, till last night."

He had listened, annoyed. In a town this size your peccadilloes always caught up with

you. Or a town any size. He had said soothingly, "Well, don't get upset over it, my dear.
Surely you could explain . . . ?"

"I did. I said we had met by accident. If
she says anything to you —"

"I'll stick to it," he told her, "don't
worry."

She said, "I don't know whether she believed me or not. But if Gram —" She broke
off. After a moment, while he waited and
the wires sang, she said, "I think we'd better
not meet, alone, that is, for a time."

"Very sensible," he approved, "if unpleasant to contemplate."

She said angrily, "You don't mean that.
You're glad. You've been for some time trying to find a courteous way out."

He said quickly, "My dear child, you jump
at conclusions, also you are talking over a
very public telephone. I've warned you
against that, repeatedly." He paused,
"Edith, haven't we been kidding ourselves?
Aren't you, perhaps, a little glad too?" he
asked.

She was silent for so long that he asked,
"Are you still there?" and she replied faintly,
"Yes." Then her voice grew stronger. She
said, "Maybe I am. Maybe I'm glad it happened this way. Or, maybe I don't care. It
was fun while it lasted," she said and her

voice faltered slightly, "but perhaps not fun enough to make up for — everything."

She hung up abruptly.

He replaced the instrument and turned. Mary was standing just behind him and her eyes were bright with mischief. She asked, smiling, "Complications in the love life?"

Justice grunted, and went over to the library table to light a cigarette. Mary annoyed him. She was so sure of herself. He said, "You look very chipper this morning."

She smiled again. "I'm about to call Steve Barton and ask him to come out. I have been given to understand, obliquely, that he's your redheaded secretary's property but I was ever a kleptomaniac. I'm so bored in this codfish town I could commit mayhem, whatever that is. But not now."

"Jenny's property?" asked Justice.

"I had it straight from the horse's mouth," said Mary, and picked up the telephone and dialed a number with which she had evidently familiarized herself earlier in the morning. "Blonde horse. Also-ran."

He was digesting that in silence when she spoke. She said, "Is Dr. Barton there? Oh . . . I'm sorry, I meant Dr. Stephen Barton. I see. Would you ask him to call Miss Hathaway when he returns, doctor? No, nothing immediate. Social, not professional." She hung up presently and Justice stood smoking, contemplating his wife's picture which stood on his father's desk.

"And what," asked Mary, "do you hear from Andrea?"

Justice was thinking of this conversation when, with apprehension, he walked into his office and found Jenny at her desk, machine-gunning the typewriter keys, and the sun bright on her hair. She looked up, smiled. "Hello, Mr. Hathaway," she said.

Nothing in her manner. Nothing at all. He felt an enormous relief and unconsciously displayed it. Jenny thought, Ede did phone him, yesterday. She thought, Well, then, what sort of game is this supposed to be, play mousy, both of us . . . or mouse and rat? She felt her heart tingle with anger but her mouth was soft, and curved. She thought, Honesty, Gram says, is the best policy. Chips down. Cards on the table.

"Well, Jenny," he said, "you're looking very perky this morning. Have a good time the other night? My father was quite taken with you. He said you were the prettiest girl he had seen for some time."

Jenny said, smiling, "Come off it — that's British Merchant Marine, at least, the last time I was at the canteen I heard a bit about legpulling and leading people up the garden

128

path. No one even notices me when Ede's around," she said sadly, "and besides, I'm only the hired help."

"You underestimate yourself," he said politely, and went into his big quiet room. Then he pressed the buzzer.

When Jenny came in, notebook in hand, he looked at her with a new interest. No shabby tweed skirt, no sweater. She wore a linen suit, lime green, and a white blouse, with a pussycat bow.

He asked, "Who is responsible for the flowers?"

"I am," said Jenny. "Everything's come out at once this year. These are the first. I stole 'em. Gram will have the law on me."

"Why?"

"Apple for teacher."

He looked at her warily. He thought, Well, here goes. He asked, "It wouldn't be a bribe, would it?"

Her eyes were as wide and clear as a child's. She said, "Why, Mr. Hathaway, I don't know what you mean."

"Mr. Hathaway," he said, "to my friends. Justice to you. Sit down, Jenny, I want to talk to you."

The offensive is half the battle. He meant to get there first, by hook or crook. Mostly crook. She thought, Not if I know it. She

129

said, sitting down, and crossing her pretty legs — although Gram said a lady never crosses her legs. If she had to cross something she crossed her ankles — "Ede phoned you."

He was considerably aghast. He had planned to say, "My dear, I understand that you overheard and entirely misunderstood a perfectly harmless conversation between me and your sister night before last. I want to set the record straight."

Two can play at honesty. He asked cautiously, "When?"

"Yesterday morning."

"And if she did?"

"So, she outsmarted me," said Jenny, and he saw that, incredibly, she was smiling.

He said quickly, "Yes, she phoned . . . She told me that you had overheard something at the club the other night and misunderstood it."

Jenny said, with a vast indifference, "That remains to be seen."

Justice leaned back in his chair. He said, and this time he was being honest, "I don't understand *you* at all."

"Good!" said Jenny. "Now we are getting somewhere."

He had expected anger, a scene, a threat even, perhaps tears. Nothing of the sort.

Jenny was as poised as a bird on a limb, and as unconcerned.

He said, stubbornly and feeling like an idiot, "Your sister and I met in Boston. Quite by accident. We had a drink together and —"

"I hope it was a good drink," interrupted Jenny politely, "and only one. Ede prides herself on her woman-of-the-world attitude. That's what modeling in a dress shop does for you. But after she was married I remember Dick telling her, 'Stick to sherry, my girl, or one cocktail. Two makes you fuzzy.'"

Justice drew a deep breath. He said, "Are you trying to tell me you don't mind — ? I was under the impression that —"

"Women," said Jenny, "love to make mountains out of molehills. They're engineers at heart. But, of course, I mind — in a way."

He was growing more and more bewildered, and looking at her as if he had never seen her before. "In what way?" he asked.

She said, "I mind because Ede's married, and to a very fine guy." She looked at him steadily, her eyes as blue as the sea beyond the windows, and as deceptively calm. "I don't want to see him hurt. He isn't in a position to defend himself — from you, or from her. What she does wouldn't be my concern, if Dick weren't in the picture. But he is. Someone has to keep the well-known home fires burning. Besides," she added, "I don't think she's really serious about you, Mr. Hathaway . . . I mean, of course, Justice. Mr. Hathaway sounds a little odd in so intimate a conversation. It has an unhand-me sound —"

He said, "Go on, Jenny."

"I interest you?" she asked. "No, I don't think so. I think she's in love with her husband. I think she's bored and lonely and you," she said frankly, "are the most attractive man in town."

"Well, thanks!" said Justice.

She said, "However, I don't particularly like you. I haven't since Saturday night. I hate being lied to. And you lied."

"I did not."

"By implication," she said serenely. "It was pretty crude now that I look back. What's your sister's name? What does she hear from her husband? What's the difference in your ages? Things like that . . . as if you had seen her only over a cup of tea up at your place, the day of the club meeting."

He said, "I'm sorry, Jenny. I'm ashamed of myself. But it wouldn't have made sense any other way, would it?"

"I suppose not. I don't blame either of

you for keeping it as quiet as you have. It isn't pretty. It doesn't put you in a very pleasant light. Nor her. Girl, Marine husband in the Pacific. Perhaps at this very moment —" She broke off. "Man, wife in England," she went on.

He said earnestly, "Jenny, I swear I never meant —"

"Who does," she asked gravely, "at the beginning? Ede is angry with me," she told him. "You are."

"No," he said, and wasn't.

"Angry," she said calmly, "because you've been found out." She lifted her hand and he saw for the first time what a small hand it was, how beautifully shaped, but somehow strong. "I don't want to know," she said clearly, "exactly *what* I've found out. Not ever. But I don't like it. And I think you'll agree with me that it had better — stop."

He said evenly, "It has."

She thought, He was tired of her, he has been for some time. She said slowly, "There was no excuse for either of you, Justice."

"No. Yet you have yourself told me Edith's excuse. Boredom, loneliness. She's young, she's very pretty and accustomed to attention. She had known her husband only a short time and their time together was brief. It must often seem almost unreal to her, like a dream."

Quote, thought Jenny, unquote. I suppose Ede told him all that, at the beginning. And, in a way, it's true. Not that it makes it better. It makes it worse, she thought. Because if you know what's wrong with you and why you want to do something you shouldn't, that's the time to run away . . . before you do.

He said, "You haven't heard my side."

"All right," said Jenny. "Time's awasting, but I'll listen."

"Thanks." He leaned back and looked away from her. He said slowly, "I met Andrea when I was in college. She was — different. Isn't your first love always different? Remote as a star, and as beautiful. I couldn't eat or sleep for thinking of her. I flunked several examinations — I was always running to New York to see her and my father almost had a stroke. But when he met her he understood. It took me quite a while to marry her. I was around twenty-five when we married. She was twenty-three. That was just over ten years ago." He paused. "I was happy for a while . . ."

Jenny asked, "And then?"

He said, "We had a son. Andrea had a difficult time when he was born. The doctors said it would be wise if she had no more children. It was a great grief to her." He added, "She was so very maternal." He looked at Jenny. "You wouldn't understand," he said, and she remembered Ede telling her, "You can't understand." Why did they treat her as if she were a child? You didn't have to go through experiences to understand them, did you? If so, there'd be few writers.

She said, as she had said to Ede, "I'll try."

"There are women," he said, "who fall in love because they want children. They don't know it. They think it's the man they want. But when a child is born all the love turns to it and the man is relegated to his proper place. He has — accomplished his mission. Andrea was fond of me. But the boy was her sun and her moon, her world and her stars. I don't mean she spoiled him. She is far too intelligent. But he was hers. Exclusively. Possessively. I didn't rate. She was not to have another child. She had therefore little use for me, except as an escort, a bread-winner, a man around the house, the father of her son." He paused, and said, after a moment, "I'm sorry, Jenny. But I have to make you understand."

Jenny was scarlet. She cursed her thin skin, the tricks and vagaries of her blood.

She could take it. She was grown up. He continued:

"When a man knows he isn't wanted, he goes where he is — that's life, Jenny. You may not like the idea but, well, it's the way things are. There were other women. Andrea didn't like it. That's funny too, but, also, life. You don't want someone, yet you don't want other women to want him. Silly, isn't it? We had a pretty bad quarrel. We were reconciled, because of the boy. I — wrote Finis to what had been a merely amusing and not very serious chapter, and we went away for a short trip. Andrea didn't want to go, to leave David. She said, if we went we must take him and the nurse. I couldn't see it that way. Anyway, she went, and he was taken ill . . ."

He paused. He said, "We got back, in time to see him die."

Jenny's eyes were suffused with tears. She didn't like this man, she disliked and even feared him. She feared him because she could still feel the pull of his attraction. But like him or not, she could think only of the distracted woman, the unhappy man, the child.

He said gently, "Thank you, Jenny."

After a moment she said, "But surely she didn't blame you?"

"Yes," he said harshly. "If we hadn't gone away she would have recognized the symptoms in time, nurse or no nurse . . . something would have been done, the boy would have lived. Or so she believes."

He sighed. "After that," he said, "we went our own ways. Her way was in the slums, working for and with children. Mine was . . . well, you can imagine."

"Seven years ago," said Jenny, and did some arithmetic in her mind. "And a little later Charlotte Granley came to work for you."

He looked at her in astonishment.

"How do you arrive at that conclusion?" He didn't mean arithmetic.

She said, "It's simple, now. Something in the way you spoke to each other the day I came to the office and she showed me the ropes . . . Friends don't speak like that, or employers and their departing employees, or even people who just plain don't like each other."

He said, "Andrea went abroad over four years ago. She has a married sister in England. Very carriage trade. My father likes to refer to Andrea's English connections. He likes Andrea too. And he's violent against divorce. Why, I don't know. My mother and he weren't happy, a divorce would have been better for us all. But he is very much afraid of open scandal. Anyway," he added, "she remained over there. For better or worse, that's my excuse. Jenny, how much do you blame me?"

For a moment she was troubled. Things were never black and white as Gram had always told her. They were gray, they were all sorts of variegations. Perfection is a beautiful dream. Strength and weakness are teammates. Courage and cravenness. She could look at Justice Hathaway and see what his life had been. But Gram spoke to her warningly. That's his side, Gram said. Do you think he won't put himself in the very best light? Be sensible, my girl. What's her side — Andrea's? You'll never know, but you must always remember that she has her — explanation.

Jenny took a deep breath. She wasn't going to be sorry for him. She spoke severely to her very young heart. She thought of Ede and Dick Ainslee. She thought, I'll play it his way.

"I do understand," she said softly.

"Thanks," he said again. "Well, that's that." He rose and came toward her and she rose and the notebook slid to the floor. He stooped to pick it up and laid it on the desk. He stood facing her, and she could feel his enormous vitality. He said, "Shall we make a bargain?"

"What sort of bargain?"

He laughed for the first time. "How New England you are," he said. "I like it very much. Jenny, I'm glad we've talked. We know each other better now."

But he wasn't quite sure. Did he know her better? He was still astonished by her attitude. Had she thrown things at him, demanded an explanation, wept, stamped out of his office, or told him off, cool and deadly, that would have been New England for you. Instead, she had brought him pale iris flowing in a tall azure vase. Instead, she had told him frankly what she thought of him and of her sister. She had said, neither had an excuse. Yet she showed no signs of shrinking from him, or offering her resignation.

What kind of girl was she? he wondered, his interest quickened. He had begun to notice her, really, at the dance, and he remembered that now.

She was unlike her sister. Ede was ardent in a curious halfhearted involuntary way. She was at one moment sophisticated — civilized, she called it, adult — and the next, in tears, hating him and herself. She wasn't integrated. Moreover, she wasn't in love

139

with him. He knew the difference. Charlotte had been.

But Jenny was ardent because ardor was a part of her integral construction. She was as young and fresh as the flowers on his desk. Laughing and funny, and grave too in a little-girl way. But astonishingly grown-up too. She was a person. If it were true about her and Steve Barton, he thought Steve was something of a fool. Mary would amuse herself with him, and then tire —

All the Hathaways tired, rather easily.

He said suddenly, "How come you aren't married? It's a time for marriage."

"No one's asked me, lately," she said.

"And?"

"Those who have," she answered, "went away to the war. I didn't say, Yes. War marriages aren't up my alley."

"I should hope not. You don't look like a potential bigamist."

"You know what I mean. All glamour and excitement and then —" She added gravely, "That's why I've been worried about Ede. I want something solid. Something I can get my teeth into."

"Block that metaphor," he told her. "When you do marry, I'll send you a present. I'll send your husband one too. A first aid kit. I'll put in a card: 'Look out for her, she bites.' "

Jenny asked, "What about the bargain?"

"One thing first. I thought that you and Steve Barton —"

"Pooh," said Jenny, "or, as Yip would say, phooey." Poor Yip. She had caught a glimpse of him this morning in Richards's office, as she passed by and the door stood open. Mr. Richards was in full spate and Yip looked pale, and hangdog.

He said, "Well, it's a good thing you feel like that because now that we are friends I don't mind telling you that my sister has her eye on him. It's a predatory eye and very attractive. At that," he said thoughtfully, "she may be able to do something for him."

"What, exactly?"

He lifted his eyebrow. "You don't sound very detached," he suggested. "Well, for instance, a hospital. He came to dinner last night. He was called away in the middle of it, but he returned and I heard him talking to her about Seahaven's urgent need for a hospital and I heard her tell him that my father might be interested. I sat in on the conversation, as did Howard Morgan, very glum, since he has his own idea about what course Mary's interest should follow. My father wasn't present. Mary may be right at that," he said thoughtfully. "A hospital built and endowed . . . in this time of high taxes

. . . and especially if it would endear the Hathaway name to Seahaven . . ."

Jenny said, "The end justifies the means, I suppose?" Her cheeks were bright and her eyes. "But," she said, "it would be wonderful."

He said, "I suppose so. Personally I don't give a hoot. I'm not in the least civic-minded. I don't believe in buying favors."

She liked him for that, a little.

He went on, "About the bargain. Another chapter's closed, Jenny. I don't think you need be troubled. Ede has closed it, and that's all right with me." He added softly, "Loneliness and boredom. Try to remember."

She said, "You might get lonely again, and bored."

"With you around to keep me on the straight and narrow?" He thought, A girl like this . . . a youngster as new as morning and as malleable as clay. Or, perhaps not. There was a stubbornness in her. You wouldn't find the way too easy. And that was half the excitement. The too-easy way led, once more, to boredom.

He held out his hand. He said, "I don't suppose you'd care to — I don't imagine for a minute that you want to be friends? That's the bargain."

"Why not?" said Jenny, and again he was astonished and a little disturbed. He thought he could read her, clear as good print. He thought he had her pigeonholed and then he found the print blurred and the pigeonhole empty.

He might have admired her more, esteemed was probably the word, if she had put her hands behind her back and said sturdily, "I think we won't shake hands. And we aren't friends."

Did she believe him to have been her sister's lover? She would never ask for chapter and verse, she did not wish to know. She had said as much. But the doubt would remain, even the belief. Yet she could tell him what she thought of the whole sorry business, yet put her hand in his as now and say, "Why not?"

No, he did not esteem her for that, being masculine, and admiring strength in a woman even while he looked for, and proposed, frailty, but it made her a good deal more interesting.

He held her hand a moment. He asked, "And now, Miss Newton, will you take a letter?"

Chapter Ten

June slid gently into July, July became August, and August put on a show. Thunderstorms, heavy evenings, mornings dawning hot as Hades, nights showing no signs of relenting. The roads were choked with youngsters, on foot, on bikes, going to beaches. People went to their ration boards and pleaded for gas as if it were water in the desert. The wind stayed offshore, the sea was glassy blue, the sun reflecting from it unmercifully.

The Nook, the Barnacle, all the out-of-town road and beach places were thronged. Kids danced there, in all the heat, to the juke boxes, girls in cottons, in bathing suits, boys in white duck slacks and sport shirts. The papers reported rising temperatures, no relief in sight. The Country Club porches and beach were crowded.

Mary Hathaway rang up one Saturday evening. The girls were out but Gram took the message. Mary would like Ede and Jenny to come up Sunday. If they would, she would call for them, about four. They would swim, and have a late outdoor supper.

Gram gave them the message, when they came in from the movies, which were air-conditioned and to which everyone flocked. And later, when Ede was lying on her bed in a thin nightgown, Jenny came in. Ede felt the heat more than Jenny or Gram. Her blood was thick and oppressed with it.

Jenny asked, "Are you going?"

"For heaven's sake," said Ede, "why not? It may be cool at least. I've avoided Mary as much as possible, all these weeks. Lord knows why. I could have been up there every day, swimming. I wouldn't have seen — him, very much —" She broke off, pushed the damp hair from her forehead. "Anyway," she said, "it's over and done with . . . I don't see why I shouldn't go."

"I'm going," said Jenny.

Ede looked at her. She said, "The whole thing was crazy . . . you made an issue of it. It needn't have been. I've seen Justice Hathaway just once," she added, "since. . . . He's perfectly happy about — everything."

Jenny said, "I know. He told me."

"He told you!"

"We," said Jenny, "have had a talk or two."

Ede was flushed, and not from the heat. She said, "You could keep out of this."

"Could I?" asked Jenny.

Ede groaned and lay back against the crumpled pillows. She said, "It's too damned hot to argue or fight. Steve will be there tomorrow, I suppose. He's always there, when he's free."

Jenny said, "Mary Hathaway's interested in building a hospital . . . for Seahaven."

"I know," said Ede. "I lunched with her after Red Cross last week —" She broke off. "But she can't build a hospital, she can't build a dog kennel . . . she hasn't a cent of her own, she told me that ages ago."

"She has interested her father. They've even sent for an architect."

"Who told you?"

"Justice."

Ede raised her eyebrows. She said, "You are very friendly with him, aren't you?"

Jenny yawned. "Why not? He's my bread and butter."

Ede thumped the pillows. "You've changed," she said crossly. "I don't know what to make of you . . . Steve and Mary . . . I'm beginning to wonder if that mightn't amount to something," she said thoughtfully. "She'd be a wonderful wife for him . . . she could put him on the top."

"In Seahaven?"

"Naturally not," said Ede; "don't be

dumb. In Boston or New York. With her connections, and her father's money — after all, she'll come in for half of it someday — Steve could become a very fancy diagnostician."

"And what about Uncle Bert?" asked Jenny stonily.

"He could retire," said Ede.

"He'd just love that," Jenny said, "sitting in Steve's penthouse and watching the world go by: the neurotic women, the debutantes with hangovers, the gentlemen who are allergic to their wives —" She broke off. Then: "Uncle Bert *has* retired, practically. He doesn't go out at all. A few people see him by appointment and once in a while Steve gets him in as consultant. He can't do more, his heart won't let him. And he hates it . . . I stopped in Tuesday night and he told me so. But he's proud of Steve. People are beginning to accept him. And what's supposed to happen to this town with both Steve and his father gone?"

"I wasn't talking about tomorrow," said Ede, "I was speaking of the future. The doctors will come back from the war."

"There were never many here," said Jenny passionately, "and none so loved as Uncle Bert. And Steve could be like him . . ."

"Why," asked Ede, "should he work his

heart and soul out, like his father, for Seahaven or any other place?"

Jenny stared at her. "Mary's talked to you
about him?"

"I told you she did."

"Is she serious?" demanded Jenny.

"About Steve or the hospital?"

"Both."

"Serious," said Ede, "about Steve. The
hospital follows. She practically told me he
was the first man she had been interested in
since her engagement was broken."

"What about Howard Morgan?" asked
Jenny. "He's up here a lot."

"Old Dog Tray," said Ede.

"I see . . ." Jenny digested this. Then she
said, "Well, maybe it would be all right.
Because Steve's changed. Perhaps he isn't
for this town. Not after Uncle Bert —" she
paused, she couldn't say — "after Uncle
Bert dies." Just saying it would hurt too
much.

She said, "What will become of Seahaven?"

"Oh, for heaven's sake," said Ede, "you
talk like a City Father."

Jenny looked at her gravely. She said, "It's
our town."

She thought of that, talking to Steve the
next day at the Hathaways'. They had done

148

quite a job on the old place, Jenny admitted to herself, sitting at the edge of the pool in her scant, black bathing suit, her face rosy bronze, her hair blazing. Wings and stables, a cabana, complete with bar, guest house, gardens . . . They had done it all the first year and hadn't spared the horses. It was a good thing they had — in the middle of the rebuilding the war had closed a door on most rebuilding, but the Hathaways, with priorities and influence, had gone ahead.

The pool was screened by trees, it was lavish with umbrellas, it was charming. The clear spring water, augmented by artesian wells, fell from the mouths of frogs and penguins.

Howard Morgan was there, as usual, the Master himself, Ede, herself, and Justice. Steve was there, long enough to swim with Mary in her very startling white suit, then he had gone again. But he came back.

He sat beside Jenny now, in a deep chair, and watched her dry her hair. He said lazily, "This is certainly the life."

"It would seem so," she said pleasantly.

He looked at her sharply. He said, "I can read what you allege is your mind. I'm becoming corrupted by luxury, am I?"

"It wouldn't be hard," she conceded.

"You're immune?" he asked.

"No," she said. "I love it. It's fun. But such a responsibility. I don't suppose you've ever read *Rebecca of Sunnybrook Farm*."

"Was that about the gal who married the man who killed his wife or something," he asked, "with a grim housekeeper in it?"

Jenny giggled. She said, "You're years ahead of me. *Rebecca of Sunnybrook Farm* was a girls' book, back when my mother read girls' books. I found it in the attic."

"Dog story?" he demanded. "Rebecca come home?"

"She was a child," she said severely, "and she had a parasol. Pink, I think. And she said, of the parasol, 'It's the dearest thing in life to me, but it's an awful care.' I probably misquote, it's been years since I repaired to the attic and dug out Rebecca and the Dinsmore books. . . . Wonderful," she said dreamily, "the attic was dry and sunny and flies buzzed against the screens and there were trunks of clothes and shelves of books and popcorn hung up to dry, and I ate apples, and read and read —"

He said, moved, "You don't grow up, dear."

It was the first time she had felt close to him. She looked up and felt the tears in her eyes. This was the old Steve. Not the Steve who wanted to lounge by swimming pools and who wouldn't interest himself in the things which happened right under his sunburned nose.

She said, "Steve, have you heard anything more about the episode at the club, Decoration Day weekend?"

"Which one? Oh, the kids. No," he said, "not much. I do think, however," he told her, "that one or the other of those places is selling liquor in a back room. I don't get the defense workers, you know. The yard has its own doctor. And the compensation work doesn't come to me. But a very scared man came to the office the other night. I couldn't find out a thing about him, where he worked or anything. He said his girl was in trouble. His very words. She was fifteen, he said. He told me she had been drinking one night — 'at one of them places.' Again, his phrase. He wanted to know what I could do about it. I told him I could give her prenatal care and deliver her, eventually, at home or over in Northam, or if that wasn't what he wanted I could tell him of a home upstate which takes girls who are having babies, keeps them, sees them through and then finds decent homes for the children. But that wasn't what he wanted either. So he went away."

"Oh, Steve," said Jenny, and her throat hurt.

He said, "He came back. She'd had an abortion. In another town. He wouldn't say where. The man had sent her home. So I went to see her and took her to the hospital. She died, Jenny. There was an investigation . . . it will be in next week's paper. But the police haven't found out who performed the butchery."

She said, "Steve, you could find out. You could find out which places are selling liquor to minors."

He said, "Jenny, the police have tried. They've gone into all the little dumps and they haven't found a thing."

"Who owns them?" she demanded.

He shrugged. "I wouldn't know."

Mary came up, sleek and dripping. She had pulled off her cap and her hair was shining jet. She said, "Steve, darling, I've good news . . . They called me to the phone a moment ago and Foster is on his way here by car."

Steve turned, his face lighting. He had forgotten Jenny, forgotten the dead girl, forgotten the juke places. Foster was the architect.

And Justice, coming across the grass to the ledge, very tall, remarkably well built, his body brown and powerful, went straight to Jenny's side. He looked over and smiled at Howard Morgan making heavy work of a conversation with Ede, said gravely to Jenny, "Shall we dance?" and pulled her out of her chair.

Steve watched Jenny and Justice executing a highly professional rhumba at the edge of the pool and Mary, glancing at him, saw that his lips were compressed and his fair brows drawn together. She said softly, "I know what you're thinking."

He replied, genuinely startled, "I hope not."

She said, smiling, "It's simple. You are watching a pretty girl in a black bathing suit dancing with a good-looking man in a pair of navy and maroon trunks. You're thinking that the performance — although executed under a blue sky and in the sunlight — is slightly indecent. Steve, you are still a Puritan at heart."

He shook his head. He said feebly, "Nonsense." But he had been thinking just that. He had thought, further, that one of these days he must have a long talk with Jenny. He listened to Justice's whistling of the tune they danced to, saw him give Jenny a gentle push and watched them both fall into the pool.

Jenny came up, sputtering and furious. "I could kill you, Justice Hathaway," she said, when she could speak, "I'd just dried my hair."

"She's such a kid," said Mary tolerantly.

Howard Morgan was applauding the little scene and Ede watched without laughter. Ede thought, Wait till I get hold of her —

She was more than ever convinced that Jenny's acute interest in her affairs was dictated by neither sisterly affection nor concern but by a motive purely, brutally selfish. Ede had seen Justice once, as she'd told Jenny. She had asked him, "Has Jenny said — anything?" and he had shaken his head. "No," he said. And then, he'd smiled at her, and said, "But you were, of course, entirely right."

His tone was regretful, but not convincing. Someone had interrupted them, as they had met, by accident, in a Seahaven shop; and the conversation had not been continued.

She had thought, It was a good out — he was glad of it. I'm glad too; I've been such an unmitigated fool.

But now life was flat again, without sparkle, without intoxication, as it had been before the day she sat drinking tea in the Tavern and Justice Hathaway detached himself from a group of men at the bar and came over to her table. There was nothing left of their brief association except a sickening sense of futility and self-disgust . . . and the frightened knowledge that when Dick came back the disgust would deepen and she would reproach herself to the end of her days. But not yet. She was, at the moment, too concerned with Jenny, and her anger against her. She had to sit by and watch this comedy played out under the summer sky and there was nothing she could do about it . . . nothing.

The Hathaways' ancient butler came down from the big white frame house with its wings and terraces and sloping lawns, and went into the cabana to officiate at the portable bar. Jenny and Justice emerged from the water, and picked up the big soft towels and found themselves wicker chairs, on which they could drip harmlessly. There was iced tea, iced coffee, and any kind of a drink you wanted. And presently the swimmers dressed and went up to the house and Justice asked Jenny, "Want to see it?" and took her on a tour of the great living room, cool and quiet, filled with flowers, the paneled library and the dining room, the sun porches. She was a little bewildered, regarding what Mr. Hathaway had wrought from the Elton farmhouse . . . a house which had stood since the early seventeen hundreds.

Steve had vanished when they returned to the others, and Mary said confidently, "He'll be back. Supper's cold, anyway . . . and out on the terrace."

The terrace was gray flagstone, surrounded by a clipped hedge. Hurricane candles glowed, as the sky darkened, and the long table was set with gay pottery and tall glasses. The manservant and a maid served, and Foster, the architect, drove in from Portland and joined the group. And after a while Steve came back and when he had had supper, he, Foster, Mr. Hathaway and Mary vanished into the library.

Howard Morgan, sitting at one end of the table with Ede, was doggedly discussing politics and Ede was listening, bored and quiet, but looking receptive. She said yes, at proper intervals, and no, with proper astonishment and indignation, and Mr. Morgan thought her a most intelligent woman and one he could go for in a big way — not that he ever expressed himself in the current patois, even in his own thoughts — if it weren't for the fact that he was irretrievably attached to Mary Hathaway. Why, he didn't know. He was a sober, solid, dull man, with a great deal of money, considerably older than Mary. He had watched her grow, fall in love and out again, he had seen her conduct herself shockingly, if with discretion, and then fall violently in love with a young man of no social or financial pretensions — some youngster she had picked up in a canteen, whose people lived God knows where and who had been a humble bank clerk before he went into the Air Forces. Morgan had suffered throughout their brief engagement, always hoping it would not last. Mary's attachments never lasted. They were brief and hot and lighted kindling wood. But the Hathaway opposition was finally conquered, and the wedding invitations sent out. They were to have been married on Pat's next leave. But before his next leave, Pat had met another girl . . . and eloped with her, on a three-day pass.

Now, Howard Morgan had thought, sitting out Mary's rage and tears and misery, she will turn to me.

But she hadn't. She had turned to no one until this — this country doctor came along with his war service and his crippled right hand.

He went on talking to Ede and Ede listened and watched Justice detach Jenny from her chair on the terrace and say, "Let's go look at the white garden."

The white garden was Horace Hathaway's

pride. It was composed entirely of white and sweet-scented flowers, which glowed in the moonlight and made a patch of fragrant light in the darkness.

It was some distance from the house, near the rose gardens, beyond the cutting beds and the perennials. They stood there, under a newly risen moon, and Jenny sighed. She said sincerely, "It's so utterly lovely."

"You are, you know," he said slowly. He had been increasingly aware of her all evening. Now he put out his hand, caught hers and drew her close. She came without resistance, her heart pounding. He said — and it was an approach which rarely, if ever, fails — "I know you don't like me, Jenny. And all you think of me is true. I'm no good." He laughed shortly. "And I've hurt you, badly, through someone you care for — I don't expect you to forgive me . . . I don't even ask it. If I had realized —" He broke off, and held her to him, suddenly, closely, bent his tall head and kissed her.

She was passive, in his arms. She did not struggle or speak. She did not respond. He said harshly, "Jenny?" and kissed her again. And she viewed herself with an enormous detachment. She thought, I don't like this man. He makes me — sick. Yet, there's something . . . It's as if he were kissing someone else and I was watching. The girl he is kissing doesn't mind, she even likes it, a little . . . But *I* mind.

Up at the house, Steve came out of the library. He had promised to look in on old Mrs. Meadows before he went home. Mary followed him. She said, "But there's so much to discuss."

"I know," he said, "but I've an appointment. I must make this call, Mary."

She said, "Of course . . . I understand."

When they reached the terrace, he looked around for Jenny but she was not there. He said, to Ede, "I'm shoving off . . . do you and Jenny want to come along?"

Mary said, "Steve, don't break up the party," but Ede said quickly, "I think we should, Steve . . . Only Jenny isn't here. She went off to look at the gardens with Mr. Hathaway . . ." She hesitated a moment and then said smoothly, "Perhaps you could find her."

Mary smiled faintly, in the darkness. She thought, Ede's being clever — she thinks.

Steve went off alone across the lawns. He wondered absently why Mary hadn't come with him, but she'd sat down on the arm of Howard Morgan's chair and was talking to him. Perhaps she felt that she had neglected him. Mary was a remarkable person. Her slight, almost unconscious arrogance amused him. It came of self-confidence, the confidence induced by the possession of as much security as money could buy. He liked her quick mind, her somewhat cynical outlook. He was attracted by her physically. She amused, and stimulated, him. She was the antithesis of so much . . . silken and sleek, and seemingly untouched by the crumbling of their world. She wasn't particularly real, he thought, striding across grass, reflecting idly that it must cost a fortune to keep it in this green velvet condition, in this heat. And so, exactly what he needed. He'd had all the reality he wanted, and to spare, during his service, and in his work, always conscious of his constant anxiety over his father.

If the hospital went through — and Hathaway seemed definitely interested — it would be marvelous beyond all dreams. He could feel alive again, working for something he wanted, which his father had always wanted, which the town needed. Damn the town, anyway. There was enough money in it to build a hospital but, no, the people were too apathetic, too satisfied. The Northam hospital had been good enough in their fathers' time, it was good enough now.

As for his hand . . . hell, he could drive a car, he could get along. He couldn't be a surgeon. Over and done with, that dream. But if they had the hospital he could expand his interests, augment his usefulness. He knew that the Hathaways would see to it that he'd become chief on medical, anyway. Perhaps he could find time for research. Next to surgery, he had always been interested in research. Allergies, he thought, there wasn't a good allergy man within a hundred miles. If —

He had almost reached the moonlight garden, and he could see Justice and Jenny. He could see Jenny in Justice's arms.

He forgot Mary, he forgot the hospital, he forgot everything in a sudden blaze of anger. What the hell was this all about? The old pattern, sordid and distasteful, the snickering, smoking-room story: "Have you heard the one about the boss and his secretary . . . well, it seems she came in and said —"

Jenny. That redheaded kid whose legs had been too long and whose tongue was hinged . . . that crazy, bubbling-over brat, with her pigtails and her freckles . . . Gram's Jenny. His father's; and in a way, his.

But she wasn't a kid any longer. She was twenty years old. She knew the answers.

Did she know the answer to this one?

Well, what happens next? You go up and say, "Let her alone." You smack the guy on the button, you turn Jenny over your knee, and paddle her little behind. You shake her till her teeth rattle. You say, "You damn-fool kid, do you know what you're getting into?"

No, you don't, not with a crippled right hand. You aren't up to Hathaway's weight or height. You aren't up to anything. And Jenny's too old to be spanked. Besides, it isn't your business, is it?

He was shaking with anger, frustration, and the awareness that everything had gone wrong . . . his home-coming, the people he had left at home now altered irrevocably . . . his father, stubbornly hanging on, and fighting for every hour of time, the town itself, and now Jenny.

He cleared his throat harshly and Jenny stepped from the circle of Justice's arms and they turned.

Steve said a little too loudly, "I have to go, Jenny. Ede thought that maybe you'd want to come along."

Jenny thought, How long has he been standing there? Her anxiety communicated itself to Justice, who put his hand on her arm briefly, reassuringly. He answered for her. He said, "But it's the shank of the evening . . . to coin a phrase."

Steve said, "I've got to make a call. Are you coming or not, Jenny?"

She thought, *He did see us.*

If so, he'd say so, sooner or later. He'd scolded and teased and exhorted her for most of her life. But it didn't matter. She didn't care what Steve thought. Perhaps, as a matter of fact, he didn't care what she did. He had other interests. And *her* interest lay in keeping Justice Hathaway's interest in her . . . until he forgot Ede existed, until Ede saw that he'd forgotten.

She said, "I'm coming, Steve," with such infuriating meekness that Steve was once more consumed with the desire to spank, but hard, and Justice grinned slightly. Jenny was developing new and more fascinating characteristics every moment.

They went back to the terrace, Justice making light conversation, asking about the consultation in the library. "I hope you and Mary will let me sit in one day," he said, and Jenny saying nothing at all. When they reached the others, Mary rose and came toward them. She said, her hand on Steve's arm, "Steve, Mr. Foster suggests that we drive up to Portland sometime soon when you can get away for a day. He's going to be busy doing a job up there, something about postwar planning. But he thought, if we'd come up, you and Dad and I, he would have some definite suggestions and possibly rough plans."

He said absently, "That would be fine."

A little later Steve, Ede and Jenny drove off. No one said much. Jenny tried valiantly. The place was beautiful, she said with enthusiasm. It was wonderful how much they had added to it, yet had succeeded in not spoiling it. She also remarked that it was marvelous that they kept their help — that aged, stage butler, the housemaids, and what a cook!

Steve said nothing, eloquently.

He dropped them off at the house. "See you later," he said.

Going up the steps, Ede said bitterly, "You certainly made an exhibition of yourself with Justice. What were you trying to prove?"

"How do you mean, exhibition?" Jenny inquired.

Ede said, "Dancing around at the pool like a couple of — of jitterbugs."

"Since when has amateur dancing been an exhibition?"

"It's not necessary," said Ede savagely, "to make with the wisecracks. Falling in the pool and —"

Jenny said, "Everyone falls in pools!"

Ede said, "You're impossible, Jenny, going off with him like that after supper."

Jenny said sweetly, "I forgot to take a chaperon."

Ede opened the door, Jenny went in, Ede slammed it. Gram came out of the living room and asked brightly, "Have a good time? Ede, you burned a little, didn't you? Who brought you home?"

"Steve," said Ede, and went upstairs.

Gram looked at Jenny. She said, "What's the matter with her and why didn't Steve come in?"

Jenny ignored the first question and replied to the second, "He had a call," she said. Gram observed that she was looking young and tired, her bright cotton frock a little crumpled and her red hair out of control, her lipstick smudged. She asked, "Have enough to eat?"

"Too much. It was wonderful."

Butch came down the stairs. She looked sleeker and fatter these days. But she had not given up hunting for her kittens. All but one had been given away. Butch had asked, "What's the use of having kittens year after year and not being around to see at least one of them grow up? It's silly. I do all the work and someone else has the benefit." To which Jenny had replied with another question, "Why keep on having them then, darling?" Butch, affronted, had replied, "But that is categorical!"

This was the sort of conversation Butch and Jenny had held for years. Long ago, when Butch was a kitten, she used to report to Steve who had affectionately opined that she was as crazy as a hoot owl. Originally the conversations were dreamed up to amuse Steve but after he went away she had kept on with them. Sometimes she believed in them.

She had therefore insisted that Butch keep one kitten, a male, striped and raffish, with a crazy little tail. She had named him Uncle Rafe after the extraordinary hillbilly baby created by Paul Webb.

"Where's Uncle Rafe?" asked Jenny.

Butch spoke purringly.

"She says," reported Jenny, "that he's upstairs sleeping his fool head off."

"You and that cat!" said Gram.

She forgot to repeat her question about Ede.

Chapter Eleven

On the following day two things happened. The first concerned Justice, coming in bright and early on a Monday morning, and the second concerned him also.

He stood by Jenny's desk and put his hand on her hair. He said softly, "It ought to burn, but it doesn't. It feels cool and rather like curly silk."

Jenny moved away from his hand. She said, "How quaint!"

Justice asked, "Have you forgiven me for last night?"

She swung around, looked up at him. She said, "There's nothing to forgive. I could have stopped you."

"Why didn't you?"

"I didn't want to," replied Jenny with perfect honesty. She watched Justice read his own meaning into that reply. She had intended him to, and now she saw him look slightly smug.

He said, "You're an honest little thing, Jenny."

That amused her very much. He added,

low, "And very disturbing."

"Good." She bent her bright head to the machine. She said, after a moment, "There are some messages on your desk."

"Thanks," he said. He lingered, however. "I'm not to mix pleasure with business?"

"That's right," said Jenny.

"Office hours are strictly office hours?"

"Roger," she said.

Justice laughed. That's what Charlotte had said too, if a little more ardently. Charlotte had said, "But, darling, we'll have to pretend . . . from nine to five."

She had thought they could; she had believed that from nine to five you could be one person and after hours another. She had been wrong. Jenny would find that out. But Jenny, he reflected, going into his office, would try to play it that way. He had tried, with Charlotte; it was Charlotte who had given up trying. But this time it must be much more discreet. His father had not been happy over the Charlotte episode, there had been a good deal of talk in the New York office and, of course, here.

Charlotte had left of her own free will. One, there was no longer any reason for staying and, two, Mr. Hathaway had demanded that she leave; since Justice wouldn't fire her, he would. It had taken a long time for Justice's father to come to the correct conclusion about Miss Granley but he had done so eventually. And from now on in, he would be less indifferent to his son's employees. Last night, for instance, Justice had seen him regarding Jenny, thoughtfully, more than once.

The rest of the day no personal word was spoken. Two men from the Navy Department arrived early in the afternoon and Justice was with them until closing time. Then he came into Jenny's room. He said, "We're going to work late. You go along home. I don't need you —" he dropped his voice — "that is, I don't need you — here."

She said, "All right, Justice."

On the way out she met Mr. Richards. He said, "I'll take you home, Jenny, if you like. Besides, I want to talk to you."

She felt slightly apprehensive. If he had heard anything . . . ? But what was there to hear? she thought, reassured. If he had, he'd say so. He had known her too long and too well not to consider her one of his family.

But it was Yip Morrison who concerned him. He said, driving toward town:

"I'm letting Yip go, after a long talk with his mother. He's signing up, with the Navy. She's given her consent. It will be the best thing that's happened to the kid. He still won't say where he and the Harris boy got the liquor that night. It's as if he were too scared." He sighed deeply. "Harris will keep a tight rein on Pooch from now on. But Yip's different. No father, and Mrs. Morrison is an ineffectual little woman. The Navy's best for him."

Jenny asked, "Have you no idea at all — ?"

"Sure," said Richards. "Either the Barnacle or the Nook, or maybe that place farther out. But they've been inspected and it's all very open and above-board."

"Who owns these places?" asked Jenny.

"A holding company," said Richards; "they've a chain of them all along the coast. They're leased to the men who manage them. There's one in town . . . they call it the Purple Parrot."

"That place?" asked Jenny, astonished. "I didn't know they all hooked together."

"They do. But more than that we can't find out. I went to the Purple Parrot myself the other day . . . There's nothing unusual about it. The routine juke box, a soft-drink bar, a dance floor. The kids from that part of town keep it crowded, even in summer, it's air-conditioned. But someone said that they understood there were slot machines in the back room. If so, I didn't see any . . . I went into both rooms, on the pretext of looking for someone. I talked to the policeman on that beat. He said it was a very orderly place, run just for the kids. I talked to the manager. He said they weren't more than making their expenses but he thought it was a civic duty to run clean, decent places where kids could go and have a good time and be kept off the streets. They close at midnight, he told me."

"Do you know him?"

"No, he isn't a Seahaven man," said Richards. "The cop — I've known him for years. He was in a jam on the force about five years ago and, while they overlooked it and kept him on the force, he never got his promotion. He has a wife and a big family. I wouldn't put it past him to accept protection money. But we can't prove anything. And at that maybe we're all wrong. Only last night there was an accident, Jenny, out by the Barnacle . . . kids in a car. The boy who was driving was drunk. I understand that the manager said that, yes, they'd been in his place, that they'd come in, behaved badly, and that he'd put them out."

"Who were they?"

"No one I know," said Richards. "They live in the new housing project. The girls

171

work in shops in town, the boys —" He shrugged. "All under seventeen and with, apparently, plenty of money. The boy who was driving was badly hurt. He's at Northam hospital. No other car was involved. The kid simply drove into a ditch. People living nearby called the ambulance from Northam and the state police. They took the other boy and the two girls to Bert Barton's office. Steve was out but Doc was there, and he had them fixed up by the time Steve came in. They were taken home."

Jenny said, "It's getting to be a problem, isn't it?"

Richards sighed. "I suppose," he said, "this is happening all over the country. Kids have more money to spend than ever before. Many of them hardly see their parents from one day to the next. School's out, there isn't even that check on them. So they barge round getting into trouble. But I'd like to get my hands on whoever sells them the stuff. Because someone does."

After supper Steve came by. He went up the steps, opened the door and shouted, "Anyone home?"

Ede wasn't. She was at Agnes Simpson's — this time, thought Jenny, she was really at Agnes's. Gram was entertaining her old friend, Mrs. Harmon, in the living room and

Jenny was writing letters.

She came tearing downstairs. She said, "I am."

He said, "I'm going to make a country call. Want to come along?"

She said she'd like to. She thought, This is where I get the works, and tossed her head mentally. It would have been easy to say no, she couldn't, she had a date, she was going to the Canteen, she had a headache, or a good book, or Gram needed her. But it was silly to stall. Get it over with.

They went off after informing Gram of their plans, and were not two blocks away when Steve said, "I didn't bring you along for the fresh air. I brought you to give you hell and then some."

"Lovely," Jenny said complacently.

He said, driving at a legal rate of speed, and wishing he needn't, "About last night —"

Jenny interrupted brightly. "I already know. Last night some kids drove into a ditch and they took three to your office . . . Steve, doesn't that make you want to find out what's going on in this town, and stop it?"

He said shortly, "I have enough to do without meddling. The kids were tight, yes, the boy told me frankly that he'd swiped a bottle from his father's supply. That's all there was to it."

"A lot of people think these juke-box places are selling it."

"I doubt it," said Steve. "They've been investigated. They are just what they profess to be, places selling soft drinks, sandwiches and ice cream, with a mammoth juke box and a dance floor. But I didn't bring you here to talk about that. I want to talk to you about yourself. And your esteemed boss. I watched you for a couple of minutes last night. Very effective. Garden," said Steve, "moonlight and roses. Hearts and flowers . . ."

"So what?" said Jenny. "So, I went walking with Mr. Hathaway and he was taken romantic and kissed me. What's so world-shaking about that?"

Steve said, "I don't understand you. You're the man's secretary. And he's married. That's the situation in a nutshell."

"Habit-forming, isn't it?" said Jenny. "And nutshell is right."

He said angrily, "Haven't you any excuse?"

"Well," said Jenny cautiously, "I suppose I could run one up on an old loom. Justice is very attractive. Also very rich. Or hadn't his sister brought that angle to your attention?"

"What has she got to do with it?" Steve demanded.

"Don't shout," said Jenny sweetly. "Nothing at all, is far as I'm concerned."

"Go on with your excuses," he said shortly.

"It's war," she said dreamily, "forcing house of emotions. I quote. Also man shortage, or hadn't you noticed? And Justice hasn't much of a wife," she said plaintively, "she's sort of worn thin after four years' absence."

He said, "I can't believe my ears. Do you mean to sit here and tell me that you expect he'll — marry you?"

"I hadn't thought that far ahead," she said. "But, now that you mention it, it's an interesting possibility."

Steve said, "I could shake the daylights out of you. You — you aren't yourself. You've changed . . . incredibly."

She said, "And so have you."

They had left the town, they were riding out on a country road. The trees were still, in the windless hot night, their heavy foliage smelling of dust.

He said, "Well, okay, so it's none of my business."

Jenny was silent, then she said, "No, it isn't. And you are making an issue of nothing. We went walking, and he kissed me. He didn't mean anything. It was quite harmless. Or do you still believe in leprechauns and Santa Claus? Have you intended marriage every time you kissed a girl?" she inquired. "That's mental bigamy. You've even kissed *me*," said Jenny, "and I don't seem to remember that you followed it up with any formal proposal."

He said violently, "Jenny, this is different. I don't expect you to reach the age of twenty without having passes made at you. But this man. Good Lord, you work for him and he's married!"

She said wearily, "The needle always sticks at that part of the record. Steve, did you ever kiss a married woman?"

To her astonishment he laughed. He said, "Several of them. One slapped me, one told me when her husband would be away on a fishing trip, and the other burst into tears."

"Well," said Jenny, "then don't be stuffy."

He said gently, "Jenny, you're just a kid. And this is a small town. People are bound to talk. I'd like to spare you that if I could. And you might . . ." He hesitated. "Tell me one thing. Are you in love with him?"

"Why?"

He said, "Because if you are . . . that changes the picture, doesn't it? Are you?"

"Nope," said Jenny cheerfully, "not in the least."

Steve stopped the car before a farmhouse, the lawn in front ragged, the lilacs overgrown. He said, "I'm damned if I know whether that makes it worse or better."

She waited for him in the darkness, smelling the scent of unknown flowers, hearing the drowsy conversation of the birds. The lights glowed in the windows and presently Steve stood on the steps talking to an anxious woman. Jenny could see her, as the light from the hall streamed out . . . a little woman in a blue house frock, an apron around her waist. Steve looked tall and thin and his voice was quiet and reassuring although Jenny could not hear what he said. She was filled suddenly with pride in him, in what he was doing. He could be a very big man, she thought, as big as his father. *If* he could see things as his father saw them.

He came out and got into the car, putting his bag in the back seat. He said, "Kid with a stomach-ache. His mother was sure it was an appendix. It wasn't. I wish to God we had that hospital," he said, sighing. "There was a kid did have an appendix the other night. I got him to Northam but it was touch and go."

She said, "Keep working on Mary and you'll get one."

"I don't like your tone," he said sharply, "but as far as that goes, if you're civic-minded, you'll use your influence with your boss."

"Here we go again!" said Jenny.

They were still quarreling when he left her at the door of her house.

Gram popped out of the kitchen. "Did Steve come in?" she asked. "I made iced coffee. Mrs. Harmon's gone."

"He scrammed," said Jenny.

Gram sighed. She said, "You two always fought, but it seems to me you're worse since he came back."

Jenny said, "He's impossible."

"You should make allowances. Perhaps he thinks you're impossible, too," Gram said.

"Maybe I am," said Jenny, and went into the kitchen to get a glass of iced coffee and a cooky. Ede came downstairs presently and joined them. She hadn't stayed long at Agnes's. They sat and talked with Gram until Ede yawned and went up to bed. And Jenny said reflectively, "Gram, I think I'm getting into trouble."

"Care to tell me about it?" Gram asked.

"No," said Jenny. She ruffled the white hair with her hand. "It isn't real trouble," she said, "just a carbon copy. Undertaken, I may add, with the best of motives. Don't worry, darling," she added, "I'll claw my way out."

She washed the glasses, turned out the lights and presently she and Gram went upstairs to bed.

Chapter Twelve

A week or so later Steve and Mary drove to Portland to see Mr. Foster. They left early in the morning and would be back that night. Dr. Barton had insisted upon it. Mr. Hathaway had been called to New York and could not go, but Foster was leaving for the West Coast the following week and wanted to discuss the plans before he left. Dr. Barton said, "I'd follow it up, Steve. I can take over for a day . . . don't worry. This means too much to us all."

Steve considered that. His father was right. He had, as it happened, no very sick patients. His father promised that Dr. Mathews would take any emergency calls during the evening.

"Go along," he told Steve, who was still hesitant. "Nothing can happen. I swear I won't climb a stair, I won't exert myself, in the least degree. I'll call Mathews, I'll simply sit here in the office and take the appointments."

Steve and Mary did not get back until early morning and at about eleven o'clock

Jenny, on her way up to bed, heard the fire signal shrieking across the town. She counted the signals and went to the telephone in the hall to look at the signal locations printed on a piece of cardboard and thumbtacked to the wall. She said, aloud, "Why, that's near the Barnacle."

She ran upstairs and burst into Ede's room and Gram called up from the living room where she was setting things to rights. "I wonder where the fire is —"

Jenny shouted, "Out near the Barnacle." She said to Ede, who was lying in bed, reading, "There aren't many houses in that district . . . Ede, suppose it should be the juke-box place. It's bound to be full of kids, this time of night."

Ede sat up. She said, horrified, "Oh, Jenny, no, that would be horrible."

Jenny flew downstairs and met Gram coming up. She said, "I'm going to phone and find out."

Living in a small town you know your telephone operator. The Newtons' wire was a party line. It was busy. Mrs. Allen again. Jenny could hear her voice, talking interminably, with no interruptions from the person on the other end. She broke in. She said, "Mrs. Allen, this is Jenny Newton. I was going to call the telephone office and

181

ask about the fire."

"Why, Jenny," said Mrs. Allen, "haven't you heard? It's the Barnacle. I'm just talking to Mrs. Dillon . . . she can see the flames from her upstairs window."

Jenny hung up. She went and sat on the bottom step and Gram peered over the banister and Ede came downstairs in her nightgown. Jenny said, "It's the Barnacle, all right."

Gram said soothingly, "Perhaps it isn't a bad fire, dear, and surely, even if the place was filled, there are plenty of exits. It's one-story, isn't it?"

"Yes," said Jenny, "and on the water. But it's just a matchbox and if the fire takes hold and the kids are panicked . . ." She shivered. Then she said suddenly, "Some are bound to be hurt . . . and the nearest hospital —" She broke off, "Gram! Steve isn't here. If the fire's bad they'll call all the doctors. Uncle Bert will go —"

The telephone rang.

Jenny ran to it, and they could hear her saying, "Yes," and then, "yes, of course. Right away."

"Who was it?" asked Gram and Ede simultaneously.

Jenny said, "Mrs. Hammond . . . she's calling for me . . . they're going out to the

182

fire, to set up a first-aid center in the nearest house. It's very bad."

Jenny had taken a first-aid course. She was a member of the Red Cross group in the town. She explained, getting out of her house coat and into her street clothes. The Red Cross car would call for her. The ambulance would come from Northam. The least injured would be treated on the spot, in the nearest house. All the available doctors and nurses in Seahaven had been called.

A few minutes later the car drew up at the door and Jenny was on the porch waiting for it. The woman at the wheel stepped on the accelerator and they drove away.

They could see the fire long before they reached it. The barnlike frame building burned like tinder. Mrs. Hammond explained as they raced along the winding sea road that the other cars had gone out ahead. They would turn the nearest house into an emergency ward, and set up their equipment in its kitchen. Coffee for the firemen, blankets, clothing . . . The doctors had already gone . . .

"Dr. Barton?" asked Jenny.

"They called him first," said Mrs. Hammond. "Steve wasn't there. He's out of town and expected back late."

They reached a place near the fire where

they could park and got out. The Barnacle was a beacon, flaming over the sea. Jenny stumbled in the road, sickened. The smoke billowed toward her, stinging her eyes, filling her throat. She heard people screaming.

The firemen were working valiantly. Several had been overcome by smoke, and were taken to the house half a mile up the road. One had been injured by a falling beam. The Northam ambulance hadn't come. It had been out on a call and would come as soon as possible. But it was a long way to Northam.

Most of Seahaven had turned out. The state police were directing cars, turning back those who had no business there. But civilians and servicemen, the men and women who had come to help and not to stand and gape, were permitted to do what they could. The nurses were there, and the doctors, pitifully few.

Jenny went to the house, up the road. Under the direction of a private duty nurse, she helped where she could. There was little she could do. They put her in the kitchen finally. The farmhouse was a shambles. The owners, a middle-aged man and woman, had dragged mattresses downstairs and laid them on the floor. Neighbors came with more, with blankets, some with cots. A boy died, as he was carried in. An unrecognizable young girl, her hair burned off, moaned continuously.

There were three doctors working.

One of them was Bert Barton. He had his coat off, his face was smudged with smoke and drawn. But he managed to smile at Jenny. He was giving the girl who moaned a hypodermic when Jenny came to stand beside him. She was very white. The odor in the little house was horrible. It would be in her nostrils, she thought, till she died.

She said, "You shouldn't be doing this, Uncle Bert."

"Doing my job?" he asked. "Jenny, get back into the kitchen. This is no place for you."

"I can take it," she said. "Isn't there anything I can do?"

"Do as you're told," he said shortly, but he smiled. The fire was finally brought under control.

The weary firemen came in and were given steaming coffee and long draughts of water and then went back to work. Everyone had been taken from the building, they said. The manager of the place was unhurt except for burns on his hands. He sat in a rocking chair, in what had been the best parlor of the farmhouse, and cried, without sound, as one of the nurses dressed his burns.

There were a hundred problems. One was that of identification.

The Northam doctors came, and the nurses, and a little later the ambulance.

It was past three in the morning, just as Steve and Mary drove into town, when Dr. Barton straightened up and looked at Jenny. The Red Cross people would stay on. Most of the least injured could be moved to their homes, others would remain here for the night. Northam's ambulance would make the several trips. The Northam doctors would take others with them in their cars.

There had been forty-two people in the building, most of them young people. Of these six were dead, and twenty badly burned. The others had escaped with minor burns, and a very few had run from the building before the flames reached them. One of the firemen was critically injured.

Barton said heavily, "Jenny, I'll take you home."

She spoke to Mrs. Hammond, who nodded. "Go along," she said, "there isn't much more you can do. Thanks for coming."

Tired, sickened, unutterably depressed, Jenny walked down the road with Bert Barton. He walked slowly, carefully. Dr.

Mathews hailed him. He came up, put his arm around the other man's shoulder. He said, "Bert, leave your car here, send for it tomorrow, I'll drive you home."

Barton said, "Thanks, I'm all right. It's been quite a night." He climbed into the car and sat at the wheel. He asked, "Has anyone said how it started?"

"No," said Dr. Mathews, "not that I've heard . . . Sure you don't want me to drive you home?"

"Of course not," said Dr. Barton, "I'm all right —" He stopped, gasped once and slumped over the wheel. Jenny cried out, and Dr. Mathews pushed her aside. He said sharply, "Call someone, get a man to help me."

Jenny ran down the road. Her heart pounded, her eyes were blind with tears. The first man she met listened to her incoherent urging, took her by the arm and ran back with her. He helped Dr. Mathews extricate Barton from behind the wheel. They lifted him from the car and laid him on the road, and people ran up, exclaiming anxiously. A man took off his coat and put it under the white head.

Mathews was kneeling beside his old friend. His mouth was compressed and his eyes angry . . . with the old anger, the old rebellion. Jenny knelt too. She said, "Is he . . . ?"

Mathews stood up. His voice was harsh, and broken. He said, as if she weren't there, "Someone will have to get hold of Steve. Bert's dead."

Steve Barton and Mary Hathaway left Portland in the afternoon. They had arrived in time for luncheon with Mr. Foster, had discussed the plans and specifications, and Foster had taken them to see several of the buildings he had designed and built and had also shown them the plans of the postwar project in which he was interested. His summer home was a little distance out of the city and Steve thought, sitting on the wide porch, how gracious and pleasant a place it was. But he was uneasy. His father had said, "Every man's entitled to one day off in ten years. This is yours."

Mary did most of the talking when the hospital plans were discussed, her dark face flashing into interest and animation. At such moments she was very nearly beautiful and Steve regarded her with admiration, gratitude, and something slightly more personal. It was relaxing, he admitted to himself, to get away from Seahaven for a few hours, away from the demands upon his time and energy. Yet, he admitted also, he wanted to be kept busy . . . so busy that every day he found himself going to bed so tired that he fell asleep almost instantly, waking only when the insistent hornet of the telephone buzzed in his ears. If he were sufficiently tired, he could forget a lot of things, they became blurred by fatigue. He could forget a beachhead in the Pacific, the smell of it, the look of the sky and water, the sound of planes, the sound of guns they carried and the bombs they dropped. He could forget the boys he had sweated to save and the boys no surgeon, however skilled, no drug, however remarkable, could save. He could forget the things he had seen and heard and felt.

Forget too, the sharp, impatient anguish of realization when he knew that his right hand would be useless to him as a surgeon. Oh, he had learned to make do with it, he could eat, he could shave, he could dress himself and drive a car. He was just a hundred per cent better off than the kids who had no right hand at all, and he had seen them, he had performed the amputations — but the fact remained that what he had wished to remain, what he had wished to become, would never be.

He could forget, too, the sense of strain under which he continuously labored . . .

impatience, irritation, which he must not betray, neither to his patients, who certainly didn't deserve it, nor to his father's watchful, anxious eyes. Hell, he said to himself, I'm as warped as my hand.

He could argue himself out of it . . . rationalize it, tell himself how lucky he was. Oh, sure. All the words, all the answers to the questions, he knew them all. But it didn't make a damned bit of difference. He did his work, and well, with every ounce of skill and knowledge he possessed and he was learning more every day. He forced himself to a genuine interest in each case, to anxiety, and rejoicing, depending on the case and its outcome. And he consoled himself with the knowledge that he was prolonging his father's life.

But the heart has to be in the healing, Bert's heart was always in his healing. Steve's was not.

So, the day in Portland was an interlude, a respite, beginning with their early start in Mary's fast, smooth-running car, which she drove. She permitted him to spell her at the wheel, because she understood it was a matter of pride when he offered. Early morning was lovely along the coast, the sea with the memory of sunrise still in it, the wet brown rocks, the creaming surf. The little towns were charming, in the sunlight . . . they were picture towns, white steeples pointing to heaven, white houses, green shutters, picket fences . . . cows grazing, a horse kicking up his polished heels and running free in a meadow . . . a startled squirrel . . . the flame-flash of an oriole's wings, a song sparrow singing from the top of a maple.

Yet, after they'd reached Foster's, after luncheon, and the discussion and the sightseeing, Steve was through, he was bored, he'd had enough.

He let Mary talk to Foster about the hospital. After all, it was Hathaway money. You must expect that they demand a very large hand in it, all of them. But now and then he made practical, professional suggestions. He did not, privately, consider Foster the man for the job. Foster had made his reputation in the building of beautiful country homes — it was he who had remodeled the Elton place for the Hathaways. He was an expert on restoration, and he restored with a loving and respectful hand. Also he built new houses, very modern, functional and fine. He had some business buildings to his credit, a bank, an office building, as well. But the nearest he had ever come to planning a hospital was when remaking a fabulous country house into a sanatorium, an expensive haven for the very tired, the very neurotic, all of whom were also very rich.

Anyway, the thing was in its earliest stages. Hathaway had given the green light cautiously: talk with Foster, have some plans drawn up, see what it will cost initially, had been his instructions. What it would cost, in the end, was another matter, as was the proposed endowment. This thing would be kicked around plenty before anything came of it. In the meantime Steve wasn't going to put in his two cents' worth of discouragement. When Hathaway was hooked, he told himself, watching Mary put her pointed, tinted finger on a rough drawing, watching her dark eyes, bright with excitement, then was the time to tear up a lot of plans and start from scratch.

His unrest finally communicated itself to her and she made the necessary graceful social gestures which would release them from the hospitality of Foster and his rather attractive but definitely simonized wife. Driving off, Mary suggested that Mr. Foster had designed the woman he married, and had had her built to specifications.

So they left, and later than they had expected, and stopped for dinner, also later than Mary had planned, at a pleasant old-fashioned inn set well back from a village street. The bar was quiet and pleasant, and the liquor good. Mary, Steve observed uneasily, drank three cocktails. They had apparently no effect upon her; but Steve, limiting himself to one, thought it would be wise if he drove the rest of the way. Not that the thought pleased him. He had learned that, despite his faithful exercising of his hand and the various therapies suggested for it, his arm ached after a long day, and his stiff fingers, which could be cajoled into doing their share at the wheel, became stiffer still.

They had a wonderful dinner, and hearty. Steamed clams and chowder, pilot biscuits and lobster, broiled to perfection, the coral beautiful and enticing against the paler, succulent flesh. A green salad, black coffee. It was very good and Steve enjoyed it, industriously picking at the wonderful meat while Mary, not at all ostentatiously, cracked the claws for him.

"The Foster lunch," she said critically, "was a little on the chi-chi side, don't you think? Mrs. Foster makes with the crystal and napery and charm, but so little nourishment! The omelet melted in my mouth and that's all it did. The salad had been breathed upon by garlic but there was so little to breathe upon. The iced tea," she added, "was good, and they evidently have a mint bed. And I like raspberries and cream, but not whipped to such a now-you-see-it-and-now-you-don't consistency. Nourishment," said Mary, "is what I craved . . . and what, God helping me, I gits."

Steve grinned. A refreshing girl, Miss Hathaway. He liked women who didn't diet, and said so. She looked at him, smiling.

"I don't have to," she said happily. "If I had to, I would, I'm a very vain woman. Did you know that I had been jilted?"

He thought she was joking. He asked, "Are you kidding?" and she shook her sleek black head.

"At the altar, brother," she said.

She told him about Pat and Steve listened. He remarked, a little awkwardly, that Pat was probably a little mental. Then he added, "As far as that goes, we're all jilted at one time or another." He told her about the nurse at M.G.H., not that he wished to confide intimately in his companion, but one indiscreet confidence engenders or deserves another, and perhaps would stem her flow of reminiscences.

Mary said indifferently, "Probably I'll never marry." She looked at him coolly. "I don't like ties," she said, "nor obligations and restrictions. Once, I thought I did. I was willing to knot the apron strings around my waist and toil over what is known as a hot stove — oh, figuratively, of course," she said, "as I had no intention of turning my back on the Hathaway interests. Willing, too, to have a half a dozen kids although I don't like children really, as they embarrass me — all of whom would look like Pat. But not any more."

He suggested gently that one day she would change her mind.

"When, as the phrase runs, I've got over it?" She looked at him over the rim of her coffee cup and her eyes laughed, without amusement. "Don't be naïve, dear," she said. "I am over it. I've recovered. And glad of it. Pat was a very mediocre young man, with a less than average intelligence but a beautiful body, and one of those faces which once seen you remember. Just a collection of features each of which was right for the other, if you get what I mean. But the whole business taught me that domesticity was not for me. I escaped by an eyelash, and a blonde at a USO — and I'm grateful."

He said, a little bewildered, "You'd make someone a very good wife."

"You, for instance?" She leaned back and smiled. She said, "I think so too — in the proper setting. A good house, a good address, a fine cook and the invitations issued to the right people, and I think you'd become a very fashionable practitioner. You pick the specialty. Diagnostician?" she asked critically, as if she were trying on hats.

Steve flushed. He said, "Not me. I'm plodding along in the home town doing my job."

She said, "That's stupid of you."

Steve looked at her a moment and in that moment saw her clear and didn't like her very well. But her appeal remained. You can dislike someone who appeals to you. He said quietly, "It's my father's job. He was better at it than I'll ever be but —"

She said, "What's good enough for your father is good enough for you, I suppose. Wonderful phrase."

He said, "Too good, I dare say."

Mary laughed, and took a cigarette from her case. She said, "You missed a golden opportunity. You should have seized it. You should have said, 'We'd make a marvelous team, how about it?' I might even have considered it, darling."

He said, after a moment, "I don't think so. The house and address, and even the dinner parties, would soon pall, Mary."

"Besides," she said, "you don't love me."

He laughed, at that. He said, "No. But I

find you very attractive."

"My situation exactly." She pondered a moment. She added, "But there are things we could do about that."

Stupid to play dumb. Steve's pulses jumped but he managed to look as if they had not accelerated, or so he devoutly hoped. After a moment, "Seahaven's a small place, Mary," he reminded her.

Well, this, he thought, is a beautiful kettle of mermaids. Not that I wouldn't enjoy an extracurricular course in biology. This middle road has its flaws. You don't remain on it long. In a situation like this, he told himself, you say yes, or you say no . . . Say yes, and Seahaven being a small town . . . what happens? Or say yes, and discover that, after all, it wasn't too brilliant an idea and bang! there goes your hospital, thought Steve practically, Say no, and it's gone too. So, what the hell?

Mary said, "I am aware of Seahaven. There are other towns, a lot smaller and quite remote. And also," she reminded him, "big cities, full of delightful people whom you don't know and who don't know you."

He said warily, "Maybe."

She looked at him speculatively. She liked him as well as any man she had met in a long time and he disturbed her pleasantly.

She said, "I'll probably end up by marrying Howard Morgan, despite my diatribe against domesticity. But, in the meantime —"

"Well?" he inquired, as cautiously as she.

"Leave it at that for the moment," said Mary. She lit another cigarette. And Steve was uneasily aware that now was not the courteous time to remind her, "Isn't it growing a little late?"

She said suddenly, "I wonder how far Justice's affair has progressed . . . with Jenny."

Steve felt as if someone had hit him, violently, on the head. He told himself, Easy does it. He kept his voice down, and colorless. He asked, "What makes you think it's an affair?"

Mary shrugged. She said, "Well, obviously, I know my brother. He doesn't play for peanuts nor, I may add, for keeps. He's married, or didn't you know?" She smiled. "Jenny's a pretty little thing. Not, of course, as lovely as Ede but at that I dare say when you grow to know her . . ." She broke off and said idly, "Ede and Justice were for a time interested in each other in an off-the-record way."

Steve felt ill. He asked, "Does Jenny know that?"

"If so, she hasn't confided in me," said Mary indifferently, "but if Jenny's as intelligent as I believe, I fancy she's had some inkling."

He said quietly, "In that case I doubt if Jenny has an affair to — as you put it — progress."

She asked, "You're angry, aren't you? Flower of Seahaven maidenhood. All that sort of thing. Demure, dimity, doves. I quite forgot that you had a proprietary interest in Jenny. Perhaps you were waiting for her to grow up?" she inquired and without waiting for a reply added gently, "Justice is by way of being a liberal education."

Steve said, "Don't you think it's time we shoved off?"

She was angry at herself, waiting for him to pay the bill, and walking out to the car. It had not been the time to mention Jenny or Justice. She should have waited. But she had wanted to find out something and she believed she had done so. It didn't, however, cause her to lose interest. Her interest was merely quickened.

Steve suggested driving, but she vetoed it. She said, "You don't think I can hold my liquor and you never take chances, do you?" To which he replied quite stolidly that he had no means as yet of measuring her capacity and that he had often taken chances when the risk appeared good.

Driving out of the village, she turned from the highway and when he asked, "Why?" she responded that it was pleasanter and also a short cut. She said, presently, as he relaxed, silent beside her, and thought of many things, none of them pleasant, "You're angry with me?"

"Not with you," he said.

"With whom?" she inquired.

Jenny, he thought, Justice Hathaway, Ede. What in hell did Ede mean by — But, he thought, it's probably not true, probably there isn't a word of veracity in it, women like this have gutter minds. Platinum gutter, of course.

"No one," he said shortly.

Abruptly she pulled off the road and stopped the car. She said, "Look, let's have it out, shall we? You think I've talked out of turn and that I have no evidence. I have plenty as far as Ede is concerned. It doesn't trouble me, as I'm fond of my brother, and I think he's had a rotten deal in his marriage by remote control. You see, Andrea left him — emotionally, before she left him, as it were, in person. They had a child and she was besotted about it. She was away with Justice, on a trip, when the child was taken ill. She always blamed him for it, being a woman of little logic. So, if he chooses to console himself, it's no business of mine. He's grown up, and so is Ede. As for Jenny, no, I have no proof whatever. I simply know Justice well enough to realize that he's interested in her and when he's interested he usually gets what he wants. I'm willing to concede that, in Jenny's case, perhaps he won't. Perhaps she doesn't like him. Perhaps she finds him unattractive. Perhaps, even if she is madly in love with him, she is too young, too frightened and too — conventional to do anything about it. Or," she said, "perhaps she's immune."

He said roughly, "I wish you'd shut up," and because there seemed no other way to effect this, he pulled her close to him and kissed her, as roughly as he had spoken, holding her in an embrace totally devoid of tenderness or affection but with a sort of violent, impatient desire and anger.

She liked it. She said, after a while, "Now we understand each other. Let me go."

They drove on in silence, and presently took the wrong turning and went for many miles out of their way. Driving through a village, looking for directions, they found the stores closed, as well as the one gas station, but an irate farmer wakened from his necessary sleep snarled instructions at them from his window and went back to bed.

It was some time before they reached the highway again and it was a little later that they had the flat and no one to fix it except Steve. It was heavy going with his hand. Mary was cheerful, and helped where she could, while admitting that she was no good at this sort of thing at all. They had a perfectly good spare, which was a blessing, but there was no jack in the car and they had to wait for a belated motorist to come along, contribute his and offer assistance.

Which was why they were very late in reaching Seahaven.

Steve drove. Mary, suddenly sleepy and suddenly bored, had permitted him to do so after the flat was fixed and they were on their way. She slept in snatches against his shoulder and he was conscious of the weight of her small dark head and of the pervasive perfume she used. He drove grimly, carefully, and at legal speed, wondering where in hell the Hathaways got all their gas. He asked her and she woke up and said drowsily, "Oh, essential industry."

"Not you," said Steve.

That amused her and she chuckled. She said, "Well, there are ways, I suppose. I don't inquire. It costs money but there it is, and I dare say it was always there . . . only the powers that be don't want us to have it.

They store it instead and make faces at us. They like to frighten the populace, you know . . ."

Her voice trailed off. Steve thought of boys in jungles and on beaches, he thought of planes and tanks and jeeps. He thought of kids who couldn't sleep, sitting in foxholes. He thought of kids who slept — for good. And he thought of the gasoline it takes to keep an army on the march and he was sick of the Hathaways.

They drove through Seahaven the shorter way, by the road which did not take them past the Barnacle, but there was still a dull and sullen glow against the sky and Steve said, "There's a fire."

Mary didn't answer.

He said, "I wonder . . ." and turned the corner and was at his own house and the other car was there too and the men were lifting someone from it. They had brought him home, as best they could. Someone in the quiet group out on the road by the Barnacle had said, "I'll go back and call Otis."

Otis was the local undertaker. He would have a — a car. But Jenny had cried out at that.

So Bert came home in the car of his friend, Dr. Mathews. Another man drove and the tears so blinded him that it was difficult to keep on the road. Jenny sat beside him and ached all over as if she had been beaten. The tears were in her throat and on her cheeks and constant in her heart. She held her hands so tightly together that they, too, ached. And in the back of the car Dr. Mathews held his friend in his arms.

So they were taking Bert from the car when Mary's car stopped and Steve jumped out. He asked, "Has there been an accident?"

Jenny got out. She tried to run, but her knees buckled. She steadied herself and walked somehow into his arms and got her arms around him and said, pitifully, "Oh, Steve, it's Uncle Bert."

Chapter Thirteen

It was days before Steve could look back and remember with any continuity the hours following his return to Seahaven. But certain things remained fixed in his memory. Jenny's slight weight against him, her arms holding him with desperation, the touch of her wet cheek against his and her broken voice in his ears . . . the sorrowful faces of the men . . . and Mattie, coming to the door, a shapeless wrapper over her nightgown . . . and her one rebellious exclamation. "Oh, *no!*" cried Mattie, and the tears poured soundlessly down her face and her features were harshly contorted.

He didn't remember much about Mary, at the time. Just that she said the things one always says, shocked and pitying, and offered to stay and help. And then, as there was patently nothing she could do, got into her car and drove away.

They put Dr. Barton to bed in his own room, where the windows stood wide and the curtains blew in the before-dawn breeze. The room was big and uncluttered and he slept peacefully in his own wide bed, the lines miraculously smoothed from his tired face. Jenny and Steve stood beside him, and Jenny's hand was tight in Steve's. Neither spoke. After a while she realized that Steve did not know she was there. She went quietly from the room, small and grieving, and someone drove her home and she went wearily up the stairs, dreading what she must tell Gram, hoping Gram would be asleep. But she wasn't. She was waiting, sitting up in bed, for the sound of Jenny's key in the lock and Jenny's step on the stair. When she heard the step, she called, and turned on her bedside light.

Jenny came in. Her face was smudged with smoke and tears, and very white. She looked at Gram and her heart was pierced with almost intolerable agony. Gram was old. She, too, one day . . .

All the things she had prepared herself to say, quietly, gently, vanished and she flung herself across the bed, and into the old arms which had never failed her and, when the arms tightened about her, and Gram asked, "What is it, Jenny — Tell me, dear," she told her, without preparation or preliminary.

And later, when the sun rose bright and heartless and the hot, breathless day began, when Ede came in to find them and to hear what Jenny had to say, Gram said, "Poor Steve . . ."

Jenny pushed her hair back from her forehead. She said dully, "If he hadn't been away . . . if he had kept Uncle Bert at home . . . if Uncle Bert hadn't gone to the fire —"

"I know," said Gram. "But you mustn't blame him, Jenny. He'll blame himself, and that's the worst thing that could happen to him. That's why I said, poor Steve . . ."

Seahaven was shocked out of its dreaming complacency. It had suffered its worst public disaster in many years and its deepest personal loss. The church in which services for Dr. Barton were held was crowded to the doors, and people waited outside, silent, in the heat . . . men and women and children, old and young. Important people came from all over the state, the governor came and members of the legislature. Classmates and colleagues came from Boston and New York. There were accounts in the New York and Boston papers and the Seahaven *Weekly* devoted the editorial page to the death of a man who, for many years, had served his community faithfully, giving without stint of his skill and his love.

As many as could followed him to the green acres high on the hill overlooking the sea. There were many flowers, most of them picked from people's gardens. The Hathaway gardeners stripped the cutting beds and Justice and Mary offered their cars to take people to and from the cemetery. Everyone, thought Steve, was very kind, but kindness had little power to reach him.

After it was all over, he went back to work, bracing himself against the sorrow and sympathy of his father's old patients. One of them said, "Well, he left us a good legacy, Steve, he left us you," and he felt humble and impotent and exceedingly rebellious. But too many said, "If he hadn't gone to the fire —"

It was natural that they should think and say it; and it was true.

So Bert Barton died, and other people died too, in the fire, and the town rallied from the shock and asked, "Why?" The investigation of the cause of the fire got under way and the manager of the Barnacle was held. No one knew exactly what had happened . . . from the evidence it appeared that someone had tossed a cigarette on a storeroom floor where there were oil-soaked rags. Someone else had picked up a bucket, thinking it contained water and thrown it on the flames. It was gasoline. A good deal of gas had been illegally stored, it appeared, on the premises . . . and there was more than sufficient evidence that liquor was stored there too, in quantity.

There were many counts against the manager of the Barnacle, but a Boston lawyer appeared in his defense, a smooth, expensive lawyer with technicalities tripping briskly from his tongue and people wondered, aloud, where the money to retain him came from.

The families of the dead and injured started retaining their own lawyers. There would be a number of suits arising from the fire but, as the manager was not the owner, the suits would have to be against the holding company which owned the chain. The manager might be culpable, personally, in so far as the fire was concerned, either he or his employees, but he was merely the agent or representative, in short, an employee of the company itself.

The town buzzed and the investigation continued ponderously, hampered by legalities and impasses, and Steve Barton went about his business of life and death. He had one brief talk with Jenny. Gram telephoned him herself — and she hated the telephone — and asked him to supper one night about two weeks after his father's death and he came, if with the utmost reluctance. And after supper, Ede vanished into the kitchen with Gram, and Jenny took Steve out on the back porch and put an ash tray at his elbow and told him to relax.

He said, "Is it as easy as that?"

Jenny said slowly, "I know what it's like for you —"

"I doubt it," he told her.

She grew a little impatient. She said, "Steve, I do. But you can't go on like this, not eating or sleeping."

"Who told you that?"

"Mattie. She's worried sick. You've a job to do, Steve."

"I am doing it."

"I don't mean that. You must find out who owns these places and put them out of business."

He was silent. He had been thinking that, for days. Jenny, misunderstanding, said quickly, "Don't you see? It mustn't happen again. Steve, what about the hospital?"

He said wearily, "I've not had time to think about it — since."

"Well, think," said Jenny. "It took a tragedy to make people realize how important it is to us all. If we'd had our own hospital, lives could have been saved —" She stopped.

He said, after a moment, "Not father's."

"Oh, Steve," said Jenny, "will you stop blaming yourself?"

"I'm not blaming myself," he said instantly, "I hope I'm sufficiently realistic —" He halted. "He wanted me to take that trip to Portland. Because it was so important to him — the hospital, I mean. It was one of those damnable things, Jenny."

But he was blaming himself: the long stay, the lingering over dinner, the trivial excitement and stimulus, the challenge, which Mary had presented — and the long way home. If they hadn't stayed at the table, if they hadn't lost their way, if they hadn't had the flat tire . . . if, if, if! If all these things hadn't happened he would have been back in Seahaven in time to hear the fire siren wail, in time to roll up his sleeves and go to work . . . and Bert Barton would be alive.

He stood up abruptly. He said, "I've calls to make."

Jenny did not go to the door with him. She heard him stop and say good night to Gram and Ede. She heard the screen door close and, faintly, the motor of the car start. She sat quite still. If he wanted to be that way, she thought helplessly, angered because she was helpless, because she couldn't be of service, because she couldn't get him interested in something not only obviously his duty, but which would release his grief and self-reproach in action. She wandered into the kitchen, a little later, and stood watching Gram replace her best glasses on a shelf and Ede take off her apron and pick up the bottle of hand lotion. And said, as Gram looked at her inquiringly, "You just can't reach him, somehow. Two, three years ago he wouldn't have been like this, he'd be out and tearing the roof off the town."

Ede said, "It's shock, Jenny," and Gram said, "You must give him time."

But, Jenny thought, the time is *now*. She said as much to Justice Hathaway, later. He had been very considerate since Bert Barton's death. They had worked together amiably, impersonally, and she was abstractedly grateful to him. And so, at the close of a busy, difficult day when he proposed that he take her for a drive and then, home, she consented wearily.

They drove out by the sea road and no wind blew, the air was still and unstirring and the gulls cried plaintively. Jenny sat beside Justice, her bright hair curling around her small face. But when he took the turn that would bring them past what was left of the Barnacle she said, "Let's not go this way, Justice," and he nodded, and took the other road, the one which led back away from the shore line and through the small outlying fishing towns, filled, even in wartime, with summer visitors . . . a road set with salt-box houses, old trees, picket fences, covered with late roses or morning-glories, and filled with the smell of salt and sea even at this distance, a winding country road, dipping in and out of villages.

She said, "What on earth is happening to the investigation?"

Justice said easily, "Why do you distress yourself so, Jenny?"

She said, "Are you crazy? It has to be put through at once."

"I don't think so. It won't happen again. The authorities have been all through the other places, I understand. Fine-tooth comb. They've found nothing. What happened at the Barnacle was — an accident. It won't be repeated. The man is being held. No doubt he'll get a sentence."

Jenny said, "You can't dismiss it so easily. What about the gasoline? What was it doing in — a bucket, in the drums on the place? And the liquor."

Justice said, "No doubt he was getting gas for his personal use from the black market. He isn't the only one, I dare say. And as for the liquor, there's no proof that it was sold on the premises."

"Two of the boys in Northam hospital have made statements," said Jenny, "that it was sold to them . . ."

Justice shrugged. He said, "Well, that's on the manager's plate — what's his name — Leslie?"

"It's on the plate of whoever owns these places," she said.

"The real estate company?" said Justice. "Jenny, you are taking this too hard. I realize, of course, that it's because of Dr. Barton . . ."

She said slowly, "Not entirely. I was there, Justice, I *saw* . . ." She shuddered and stopped. After a while she said. "All those — kids . . ."

He took his hand from the wheel and put it over hers. He said, "I'd like to hear you laugh again. Do you realize that there are a great many things we have still to say to each other? Unfinished business," he reminded her.

She moved her hand, and he put his back on the wheel. He said, "I can wait . . . I'm a singularly patient man."

She said, "It's late. Let's get back to town."

The past days had almost erased her complicated relationship with her employer from her mind. Driving back in silence, she thought that it had almost erased her trouble over Ede as well. Her own absurd little plotting seemed remote and theatrical. Little sister gallantly sacrifices self for misguided older sister, she thought. And that's stupid.

Ede was a grown woman. She had to make her own decisions, commit her own sins and suffer her own penalties. All Jenny had succeeded in doing was to frighten her . . . and fright is scarcely a firm basis for morality. Well, a basis perhaps, sometimes, but it had to go beyond that, thought Jenny. Besides, she knew — and had known as long ago as the Country Club dance — that Ede's affair with Justice was on the way out before she, Jenny, had known of its existence. Not from any moral reason, but because Justice Hathaway was tired of it — and of Ede.

He said, at this juncture, "A penny for your thoughts . . . the good old-fashioned kind, which doesn't look like a dime."

She said, "I was thinking how dumb I've been!"

His heart quickened. He asked cautiously, "Not about me, by any chance?"

"Yes," said Jenny. She was so tired she didn't care what she said. She thought, I may as well set him straight, once and for all, and if it costs me my job, well, I'll get another.

He asked, "Are you thinking of the other night, in the garden?"

The other night? A year, a world away.

She said, "Not specifically." She laughed shortly. "When I was a kid," she added reflectively, "I was always making up stories about myself, in which I rescued people from runaway horses or from drowning or something. Always the heroine."

He was silent. Then he asked courteously, "Whom have you been rescuing lately?"

"Ede," she said. "Oh, you know . . . it's just occurred to me that I needn't have bothered. Whatever there was between you, it's gone, and has been for a long time. Certainly, on your part; perhaps, on hers. I wouldn't know. But I would barge in, full of zeal and nobility, and try to prove to her that once a wolf always a wolf. Little Red Ridinghood," said Jenny bitterly.

He said, "I'm trying to follow you, but not getting very far."

Jenny said, after a moment, "It sounds so utterly fantastic. I thought if I could prove to Ede that you could be interested in me — too . . ."

"Say no more," said Justice, and laughed with astonishment. "So it was just a redheaded herring across the trail, and you don't like me any better than you did before."

She said thoughtfully, "Funny thing, but

I was a little in love with you . . . oh, in an adolescent, pleasant sort of way . . . like having a crush on a screen hero or even your high school teacher . . . that is, before the night at the Country Club."

"And then?" he inquired. "You fell out."

"I fell out."

"Well," said Justice, "this is interesting."

She said, "I don't think so, not any more. You and Ede . . . well, it was never up to me. I could register disapproval, disgust, all the things I felt but . . ." Her voice trailed off. She said, "I'm a dope. If Ede wanted to mess up her whole life for something that wasn't worth a damn to begin with — well, that's her business. The people concerned in it are herself and you, her husband and, I suppose," she added, "your wife, although as she's never been awfully real to me, I suppose she was even less real to Ede. As her sister, all I could do about it was hate the whole business from my heart and be sorry . . . and stand by. If she had needed or wanted my help she would have asked for it. But no, I had to see myself in the angel-from-heaven role . . . I don't any more."

Justice said, after a moment, "You're making a mistake, Jenny."

"Oh," she said, "I suppose so. It's habit-forming, isn't it?"

He said, "You've said the one thing which, being honest and uncalculated, is enough to persuade me that I am really falling in love with you . . ."

Chapter Fourteen

Jenny went slowly up the steps of her house. She thought, Too much happens, it's more than a person can take. She walked into the hall and found Butch sitting on the lower step of the stairs, industriously washing her furry, triangular face. Jenny bent down and scratched her ears. Animals were wonderful, she thought, so uncomplicated. "Where's your son and heir — ?" she began, but before Butch could answer, Jenny broke off, listening, her heart plummeting, she could hear the unmistakable, frightening sound of heartbroken weeping.

She ran into the living room. "Gram," she called. "Gram!"

The sound came from the kitchen. The dining-room table was set but no one was there. Jenny pushed open the kitchen door and saw Ede sitting at the scrubbed white table, her head on her arms. Gram stood beside her, little and thin, her face worn and frail, graven with lines of old sorrows remembered and new sorrows lately encountered. Her hand was on Ede's gold-silk hair.

On the kitchen table, Jenny saw a yellow oblong of paper.

The kitchen looked as it always did at dinnertime. It felt the same. The kettle sang from the stove, the plants bloomed on the sill. There was the fragrance of good cooking.

Now it darkened before Jenny's eyes. She said, standing at the door, "*Not Dick . . .*"

Gram looked up. She had been so intent she had not heard Jenny call or come in. She said quickly, "He's wounded, Jenny."

Jenny's heart rose . . . a wound could be, it must be, slight. It sank again, a wound could be serious . . . and fatal.

She went over to Ede, dropped on her knees beside her and tried to take all of her in her arms. She kept saying, "Ede, I'm so sorry . . . so sorry . . ."

Ede lifted her head and looked at her sister. Her eyes were swollen and her face devastated, the delicate skin blotched. She asked, "How do you suppose I feel?" she turned away, her head down again, and was quiet, but her body shook. And Gram said, "Get her upstairs, Jenny, I'll call Steve."

Ede didn't want to go upstairs, she didn't want to do anything, except sit there and weep until no more tears were left. But Jenny coaxed her to her feet, and out of the kitchen and finally, slowly, draggingly, up the stairs. She helped her undress, slipped the nightgown over her head, and turned down the bed. She watched her get in and went to the bathroom to run water for a hot-water bag. Ede's feet were like ice. Jenny talked, stubbornly, all the time. She said, "It may not be bad, at all. You'll hear in a few days. They'll bring him to a hospital here, as soon as possible and then, when he's able, he'll come home."

Ede did not answer. But once she said, "I've been such a fool, Jenny . . ." and once she asked, "If he — if he lives, do you think I can make it up to him?"

Jenny said, "Of course you can." But words didn't mean anything. She was sitting by the bed, much later, with Gram when Steve came in. He came up the steps two at a time, Gram went out to meet him and Ede said childishly, "Who's that?"

"Steve," said Jenny.

"I don't need a doctor," said Ede . . .

"Of course you do," said Jenny. "Anyway, this isn't just a doctor, it's Steve. He's been through this himself. He knows what it's like —"

She could hear Steve speaking through the half-closed door: "— couldn't get here before — caught me at Hathaways' . . ."

He came in, nodded at Jenny with his familiar lop-sided grin, the grin she knew so well, which said, Take it easy; keep your chin up . . . I'm here, and sat down in the chair from which she had risen. He took Ede's hand. He said quietly, "Bad luck, old girl."

Ede's mouth quivered, and the slow tears seeped under her eyelids. Steve said, "You must be patient, dear. From the wording of the telegram I would judge that it isn't very serious. He'll have the best care in the world. The most skilled attention, and miracle-working drugs —"

He went on talking, his eyes on her bloodless face. Her pulse ticked under his finger. Her hand was cold. He spoke to Gram. He asked, "How about an extra blanket?"

It was a hot evening, all the past weeks had been breathlessly warm, but Ede was shivering. Her teeth chattered. Gram brought the blanket. Jenny said, low, "I put a hot-water bottle at her feet."

"Good," said Steve.

Later he rose and took Gram into the hall. Jenny stayed where she was, tucking the blankets around her sister, holding Ede's hands in hers. The ceaseless shivering went on. Jenny asked softly, "Do you feel warmer?" and Ede moved her head on the pillow. Her eyes were closed. Jenny went out in the hall, and Steve was just coming back, and Gram was on her way downstairs.

She said, "She keeps on shivering."

"Shock," said Steve. "Nerves. Gram's going to bring her some broth, and I'll leave a sedative. You can call me tonight if you need me. Otherwise I'll be back in the morning." He looked worn and tired. He put his hand on her shoulder. "It may not be as bad as she fears," he said. "Let's hope not."

"Everything happens," said Jenny. She twisted her hands together. "I —" She looked at him and he seemed, as he had once seemed and for so long, strong, competent and unfailing. She asked, "Can't you stay?"

He shook his head. "I'm sorry," he said. He smiled, touched her shoulder again. "But I'll come back, I promise." He gave her a little shove, and went into the room, and she followed. He stood looking down at Ede. He said, "You'll feel better soon, Ede. Gram's bringing you some broth —"

She made a gesture of sick distaste and he said gently, "I'm not going to ask you to eat . . . just to drink something hot. And afterwards, to sleep."

Ede said faintly, "Sorry to be such a nuisance," and Jenny's eyes, for the first time, filled with tears.

At eleven o'clock Ede was sleeping. Gram

and Jenny took turns staying beside her. They had made a very sketchy meal, first Gram, then Jenny, and when Steve came again Jenny was telephoning. As he entered the hall she was replacing the instrument on its cradle. She said, "That was Dick's mother . . . she's wonderful, Steve, she's taken it so well. All the circuits were busy. I couldn't get her until a few minutes ago. She was trying to call us, too."

He nodded. He asked, "How's Ede?"

"Sleeping. The first cup of broth wouldn't stay down. Gram waited awhile. Then she tried again . . . just a spoonful at a time. That was all right. Then she waited a little longer and then gave her the medicine."

He said, "I'll just look in on her and talk to Gram. You stay there, Jenny."

When he came down again, he looked satisfied. He said, "She'll do. She'll sleep all night. Can you sleep in there with her, Jenny, on the couch? I think she should have someone close at hand in the morning when she wakes up. That will be a bad moment, when she remembers."

She said, "All right, Steve, of course. You look so tired. Can't you stay a moment? I'll make some coffee."

He hesitated. Then he said, "I'd like to."

They went into the kitchen and Jenny

measured out coffee and water and put the percolator on. They sat at the kitchen table and she said, "If only it isn't too bad . . ."

"I know." He added as he had to Ede, "You must be patient."

"That's easy to say," said Jenny with a spark of spirit.

He nodded. He said, "It's always easy to say from, so to speak, the other end. Nevertheless, it's true. Jenny . . ." He hesitated and she asked, "Well?"

He asked cautiously, "What is troubling Ede?"

"Well, *really!*" said Jenny, staring at him.

He said, "I've known her all her life. She's high-strung, and a little temperamental. Impulsive, stubborn. We both know her. I needn't analyze her to you, Jenny. But this isn't like her . . . tears, yes, grief, and the terrible anxiety. But Dick isn't dead, he isn't missing. He's wounded and I've said I feel that it isn't — barring complications — very serious. Naturally, we're in the dark, for the time being. But this complete collapse, it isn't like Ede as I know her. There's something behind it . . . something which intensifies the normal emotions."

Jenny said, "Why? Isn't it normal for her to go to pieces? I would."

"I don't think so," he said gently.

"Well, then," she said, with a flash of her old argumentativeness, "if I wouldn't, how do I know how I'd act? It's because we're different."

He said abruptly, "Something is troubling her, something she's been suppressing, and this bad news has brought it to the surface. Is it because she feels a sense of guilt . . . because, possibly, her recent behavior hasn't been exactly exemplary?"

Jenny was scarlet. She said, "I don't know what you mean."

"Yes, you do," he said, and looked at her gravely. He added, "It seems so strange . . . a year or so ago you would have come running . . ." He broke off. He added, sighing, "We've all changed."

He thought of Ede and her shallow, fast pulse under his fingers, her shallow, light respirations, the touch of her skin, cold, damp . . . the sunken look about her eyes and bloodless mouth. A moment ago when he had looked in on her her color was better, she was warm, she slept deeply. But, tomorrow?

He said, "There's been gossip about her and Justice Hathaway."

Jenny said violently, "There is only one person who could have told you that. Mary Hathaway. And she pretends to be Ede's friend! And there was no gossip."

She looked at him with hostility. He was in the other camp, or he would not have listened to Mary. She thought, Mary was Ede's friend . . . I'm glad she isn't mine!

Steve said, "Never mind where I heard it — it doesn't matter. What matters is — is it true? Because if it is, it explains a good deal. Ede," he said reflectively, "isn't the type who could take that sort of thing in her stride. She's restless, easily bored, she made a wartime marriage with a man she knew only slightly and their time together was short. Almost anything could happen and, perhaps, did. Some women could rationalize it. Ede has too much of Gram in her." He smiled, without amusement. "If this is so, Jenny, she'll have a more difficult time . . . the waiting, the not knowing, the anxiety will weigh more heavily on her. If she loves Ainslee and I assume she does?"

Jenny said, "Of course she does!"

He said after a moment, "You say it without much conviction . . . or as if you were trying to convince yourself. Because you can't understand that a woman married to the man she loves — Ede, to be specific — could for a split second even contemplate infidelity — if only mentally. You'd defend Ede hotly, naturally, no matter how you felt about it. But you wouldn't understand and you wouldn't condone. As for Ede, she's more like you, I suppose, than anyone would imagine, knowing you both. She'd defend herself — but she wouldn't understand either, and she can't, secretly, excuse or condone. She's been keeping all this under, Jenny, and the shock of the War Department wire has released it."

Jenny said after a moment, slowly, "I haven't asked how far — it went. I don't want to know."

"I can understand that," he said. "Jenny, she'll work this out by herself. One way or another. You'll just have to stand by."

Which was the conclusion she herself had come to, recently. She nodded, and after a moment rose to look at the coffee. He watched her in a companionable silence, as she stood by the stove, her red head bent. It was quiet in the kitchen. The clock ticked and Butch, who had followed Jenny downstairs, slept with one eye open in the corner. Quiet and peaceful and seemingly remote from war and sorrow and bewilderment.

Steve had been at the Hathaways' when Gram called. Mary had sent for him. She had had a letter from Foster. Her father was not home and Justice had appeared briefly and then disappeared again with too great a display of tact. Mary had been very charming and provocative, but he had felt — well, call it disinclined. They had talked of the investigation of the fire, or rather he had talked, and she had dismissed it, more or less perfunctorily, as a dreadful thing, too unpleasant to discuss . . . adding, however, that it had focused the attention of the townspeople upon the need for a hospital. Her father, she said, was going to the selectmen and suggest a town meeting at which the offer could be made and openly argued. Here she had added, her eyes smiling and her mouth grave, "That's what you want, isn't it?"

Now Jenny said, turning from the stove where she had been watching the coffee perking, with its comfortable bubble of sound, "It will be ready soon, Steve. I did want to talk to you about Ede. But I couldn't."

He thought he could understand her reason for not confiding in him and unfortunately said so. He asked, "Because you yourself were involved?"

She had picked up the coffeepot, and now she set it down as if it had burned her. "What do you mean by that?" she demanded.

"Have you forgotten," he asked quietly,

"that I saw you — that Sunday evening?"

For a moment she had. Now she remembered. She said, "But —"

"Never mind," he said, "you don't have to explain yourself to me. It's perhaps natural. You are thrown with him every day, and he is a very attractive man . . . I suppose. An exotic type," he added, "for Seahaven. But how you could —" he hesitated — "knowing that Ede . . . or perhaps," he added, hopefully, "you didn't know?"

She said stonily, "I knew."

She took the pot from the stove, poured the coffee, and fetched sugar and cream. It was hot, and good, if perhaps not quite strong enough. Steve stirred his without enthusiasm. He could understand Ede, from a more or less clinical standpoint. But not Jenny, never Jenny. She was too close to him, or had been. He found himself grateful that if his father had had to die, he had gone without hearing the gossip, without knowing. It would have hurt him very much. He was as fond of Jenny as if she had been his own.

He said, "I thought you had such a level head under that crop of crazy red hair . . . I — Oh, hell," said Steve gloomily, "you're the last person in the world to go off the deep end because a man has broad shoulders and a million bucks — particularly as he has a wife already."

She said furiously, "I don't care what you think!"

"That's obvious." He rose, his coffee half drunk. He said, "I'll shove off now. Phone if you need me. I'll stop by in the morning."

Jenny sat where she was and stoically drank her coffee, which, as she took it straight, was scalding. Steve walked round the table and looked down at her. He said, "I've made you sore. I didn't mean to — I thought, maybe, I could help. If you are in love with him —" he added mentally, Ede or no Ede —

She said, "Steve, don't be *stupid!*"

"Sorry," he said stiffly and walked out of the kitchen, out of the house. Jenny sat looking into her coffee cup. If he hadn't said what he had she would have told him the whole story. She wanted to tell him. But it was so silly — so childish. She could have told him, a year or so ago. But things were different now. Steve was different. And Mary Hathaway —

She rose, picked up the cup, and dropped it. And the coffee was a sudden dark stream on the linoleum. Picking up the pieces of the cup, getting a cloth to wipe up the spilled liquid, the tears ran suddenly down her cheeks. It was the last absurd straw. She was very sorry for herself, sorry for Ede, for them all. Everything was mixed up and burden-some, everything was *wrong*.

She put the kitchen to rights. She told herself, I can't be bothered with *me* . . . I've Dick to think about — and Ede.

Chapter Fifteen

The days dragged by. Ede got up on the third day and went about her business, which consisted mostly of sitting with an unread book in her hands. Jenny could not arouse her interest, nor Gram, nor even Steve. Mary Hathaway did, though, coming to the house, saying, "Nonsense, of course you'll see me, I've come to take you for a drive." She was brisk, pretty, and entirely practical. Sympathetic without running over at the mouth, as Gram expressed it. She bore Ede off, and brought her back again after a drive and a high tea at the Hathaway house. Ede returned looking rested, or at least a little less strained, her color was better and Gram said grudgingly, "Maybe I've misjudged that young lady. She seems to have sense."

She had more than sense, she had influence . . . Justice and his father had very higher-up connections. The telephone and telegraph wires were hot, and there were ways and means of finding out. So the Hathaways found out, for Ede. Dick Ainslee had been wounded in the shoulder and the thigh. The wounds were not serious, the new drugs precluded infection. Eventually he would be brought to a hospital, probably on the West Coast.

Ede was very grateful. She told Jenny and Gram so, over and over. She said, the evening Mary telephoned her the information, "I wonder —" she looked at them appealingly — "would you mind very much if I went out to Dick's mother?"

Gram drew a sharp little breath and Ede took her cool old hand. She said, "I know. But she's alone, Gram . . . out there, waiting. She hasn't anyone. She wrote me," said Ede, flushing a little because she had not shared the letter with Gram and Jenny, "and asked me if I would consider it. She has that little apartment in San Francisco and a room for me. We could wait there together and then if Dick is sent to the West Coast . . . Don't you see?" she asked.

Gram nodded. She said, "I see." She rose stiffly from the straight chair in the living room. She added, "If you want to go, you should. And it sounds sensible to me, Ede. Of course you take a chance on his not being sent there but meantime it would comfort Mrs. Ainslee to have you to help her over the waiting." She smiled, her blue eyes kind.

She said, "You do as you think best, dear."

When she had left the room, Ede looked at Jenny.

"She hates having me go," she said miserably.

"Naturally," said Jenny, "we'll both hate it, but it does make sense."

Ede said restlessly, "It makes more than that. I — I can't take it here, Jenny. I keep remembering . . . I —"

"Don't talk about it," Jenny said quickly.

"I have to, I won't again. Just this once. You see, at first, well, after last spring I was so resentful — of everyone and everything. You, mostly. I believed a lot of things. But lately I've been thinking. You're such a — a goof, Jen, getting yourself into silly situations because you thought you could help me. It's clear enough now. Then I got so I didn't mind seeing" — it was hard for her to say his name — "Justice, after a while. It was as if none of that time had ever been. But after I learned about Dick, it was hard again. I've even hated being grateful to him. I've been glad he's been away this past week and I needn't see him when I had to go up to the Hathaways', I could just tell Mary to thank him for me. So," she said, "if I go away . . . You understand, don't you?"

"I understand." Jenny leaned forward

from her corner of the couch. "Ede, for heaven's sake don't tell Dick anything," she advised.

Ede grew very white. She said, "I've been thinking about it, every day. Whether I should."

Jenny said, "He's had a bad time. He has to get well without anything to trouble him. He can't, if you tell him. You'll want to, perhaps," Jenny said painfully, "it might make you feel better. But it won't help him. Can't you start again from here?" she asked. "If anyone has to suffer, it had better be you," she said, low, "and not Dick."

"Honesty . . ." began Ede.

"You didn't think about that before," said Jenny, "did you? It isn't going to help now. Dick has a right to come back to the sort of life he's been dreaming about and the wife he remembers. The wife he believed in . . ."

Ede said after a while, "I don't know what will happen. Maybe he'll go back to war . . . as an instructor here or something. I could follow him. Maybe he'll get a medical discharge and go back to civilian life. He'll want to stay out in California, that's his home."

"All the better," said Jenny cheerfully.

Ede said, "All right, I won't tell him. But *is* it all right, Jenny, is it?"

Jenny said, "I don't know, Ede. I can't

seem to think about it that way, whether it's right or wrong, ethically. Only what's right for Dick."

The short time before Ede left for the Coast was crowded. The investigation into the circumstances of the Barnacle fire was concluded, the holding company, which owned and leased the various buildings, was heavily fined and, despite all the lawyers could do, the manager of the Barnacle was recommended for trial for criminal negligence. The wrecking crew descended upon the Barnacle and tore down what was left of it. And when the courts opened again, presently, the damage suits would start.

Justice Hathaway came home from New York and Washington. Production was not slackening with Allied victories in the various theaters of war. He brought with him future plans and pressing present business. Jenny, working late one evening, was not aware of the time until he came in and stood at her desk and looked down at her.

"Call it a day," he suggested.

Jenny looked at her clock, startled. She straightened up and sighed. "Golly, I didn't know the time. I've a kink in my back at that, and feel a little wilted," she admitted.

He said, "I have to stay, but you cut along home." He gave her a little pat on the shoulder. He added uneasily, "I hear Ede's going out to the Coast. Mary told me at breakfast."

"That's so," said Jenny. She hadn't mentioned it to him. It wasn't his business.

When she reached home Gram had a cold supper waiting. It was still very warm, as it often is around Labor Day. Ede had had supper and gone out to say good-bye to some of her friends in town. Jenny, with a tray on the back porch, grinned at Gram. She said, "I'm sorry I didn't phone, Gram. I clean forgot."

"That's all right," said Gram, smoothing her apron. She added, "Ede seems a little more cheerful, doesn't she? I suppose it's — well, doing something. Packing, planning. Getting ready to move. Anything's better than inaction and waiting."

Jenny said, "I guess so. Gram, don't look so sad. You've got me."

Gram said, "I wasn't being sad for myself. I'm glad Ede's going." She added after a moment, "She's too used to us, Jenny. And there's nothing for her here. Mrs. Ainslee, now, that will be different. She's Dick's mother. She can talk to Ede about Dick, what he was like when he was a baby and a little boy and a young man growing up. And Ede will have to think of her. She'll even feel a little responsible for her. Mrs. Ainslee isn't young, she hasn't been very well, and she's alone except for a servant in that apartment. Ede can take over, run the house, do things for her. She can't here," said Gram stoutly. "*I* run things. You're busy, and self-reliant. She needs to be taken out of herself. She's selfish," said Gram, "she always has been. Maybe we've spoiled her."

Jenny said, "We'll have to do a bit of budgeting, darling."

There was that factor to be considered. Ede had forgotten it, apparently. Jenny hadn't.

"We'll manage," said Gram, "just the two of us. I'll miss her ration book though," she said unexpectedly.

Even if Ede remembered and offered to send money home from the money Dick sent her, Gram wouldn't take it, thought Jenny. And she had occasion to think about it again, later.

She was upstairs, wearing a very scant pre-war robe of faded silk, when Justice Hathaway's car stopped at the door and Gram went out to see who was calling. Jenny heard them talking in the hall and Gram called, "Jenny, Mr. Hathaway wants to speak to you."

Jenny said, startled, "Half a minute," flew into the nearest garments, scrambled into a dress and dashed downstairs, her hair standing around her head in thick, just brushed curls. Justice looked up at her, smiling. He said, "I'm sorry, Jenny, I've got to go back to the office. I just had a call from Washington and there's something I need in the files . . . also I've got to get a letter out — I can't discuss the matter over the phone or even by wire — I'll drive to Northam and meet the express with it."

Jenny asked, "You want me to go with you?"

He said, "I wish I could say no. But there's no one else I can trust with this."

She said, "Okay," briefly.

Gram said comfortably, "Run along, Jenny."

But her eyes, watching them go down the steps together, were troubled and when a little later Steve dropped by, calling in the hallway, "Anyone home? How about some iced tea?" he thought he had never seen her look as lonely.

"Where's everyone?" he asked.

She told him. Ede was calling, she said, Jenny had to go to the office.

Steve sat on the kitchen table, drank the tea she produced from the icebox, ate a cooky. He said, "She did, eh? Highhanded young man, Mr. Hathaway."

"I gathered it was very important."

"Could be," said Steve. "I don't like the guy, that's all."

Gram said, "I understand you like his sister." She remembered that only a day or so before Ede had said, reflectively, at the dinner table, "I wonder if Steve's serious about Mary Hathaway — or vice versa?"

"Oh, sure," said Steve, "She's all right — in her way." He grinned. "Too rich for my salty blood though, Gram," he told her. "But she was a help. You know, when I got back here I was pretty sore about a lot of things. I needed a lift and the people who had known me and what I'd wanted for myself, well, they just didn't rate as far as helping was concerned. What I needed was someone new, who hadn't known me, who wasn't specially sympathetic, who didn't go around poor-Steveing me."

"We didn't!" said Gram indignantly.

"Yes, you did too, all of you, if only in your minds. . . . Well, that was Mary," said Steve, "a shot in the arm." He smiled, then sobered. He said, "I've been doing a lot of thinking. Since the fire particularly. My place is here and no more griping about it. I've got a lot to live up to and I'll try."

Gram said, "Of course," indulgently, confidently. She added, after a moment, "This investigation —"

"Didn't get far," said Steve. "Right. But I've done a little snooping on my own account . . . or had people doing it for me, in various places. Boston, New York . . ."

Gram's eyes snapped. She said, "You've something up your sleeve."

"Not much," he said; "yet, I think, almost enough. You coming to this special meeting, Gram?"

"About the hospital?"

"Yes."

Gram said, "Of course, I always attend the town meetings."

"You'd better be at this one," he said grimly. "It's been postponed until Mr. Hathaway could produce a fairly complete plan, with facts, figures and suggested financing. It ought to be interesting." He slid off the table. "Thanks for the tea," he said. "Mattie mustn't hear about it. She keeps it for me with sprigs of mint in a dish. But I wanted to see Jenny. Tell her so, will you? And of course I'll see Ede before she goes. It was wise of her," he said, "to make this decision. But hard on you."

Gram said, "I won't be alone. Mrs. Ainslee is, you know. I have Jenny, as she herself reminded me tonight. I have you too."

He put his arm around her, and bent to kiss the top of her white head. "You'll always have us, dear."

Jenny and Justice drove to the shipyard and went past the waiting guards. There was a big job under way, and the night shift was working. They went on up to the office, the files were unlocked and the information which Justice needed was produced. There was more in the great steel safe. He took all the folders to his desk and went to work on them while Jenny waited, in his office.

He had said little on the way over except to apologize to her for bringing her. He said, "If anyone could read my execrable handwriting, or if I could type with more than two faltering fingers, I wouldn't have brought you out."

She said, "That's all right."

It was a long report which he dictated to her after a while, and she took it directly on the typewriter. There were figures and statistics and considerable important information. She typed it as he read it to her, and later took down the accompanying letter in shorthand and typed that. He signed the letter, and Jenny addressed and sealed the envelope.

He said, "You'll have to drive to Northam with me, Jenny. I don't want to lose time taking you home and I don't want you going home alone at night."

"But —"

He said impatiently, "For heaven's sake, it won't take any time. I'm going to give this to a man on the train. It's all been arranged. He's on his way down from Portland. The train stops five minutes in Northam. He takes this through to Washington, personally."

They covered the distance to Northam at, Jenny thought, rocket speed. She held on to her hair mentally and hoped that they'd get there. They did, the train was just in, and a man in uniform was standing on the platform near his car, looking up and down.

He saw Justice and waved, and Justice ran down the platform and gave him the envelope. They stood talking a moment and Jenny looked at the crowded train. Soldiers leaned from the windows, and sailors . . . she saw WACS and WAVES, SPARS and women Marines. She saw tired boys standing in the aisles, sitting on upended luggage, she saw them crowded into the seats. She saw them sleeping, their young faces drawn.

Her heart tightened. All these boys were going where? Returning when?

The conductor signaled, and the Navy man jumped back on the train and the train moved out, slowly, and some of the boys waved to Jenny. Perhaps one of them would remember her at another time, near or distant, in another place, another station, a strange camp, aboard a troopship, in a plane. Perhaps one would remember, without rhyme or reason, a girl with red hair, a girl in a blue and white checked gingham dress standing under the naked station lights on a platform at a strange station . . . perhaps he would not even remember the name of the station.

Justice came and took her arm and they moved toward the parked car. He said, easing himself into the seat, "Well, that's that, and we have a day or more. Thanks, Jenny."

"That's all right."

He drove back slowly, sedately. And Jenny sat beside him curled up, her head against the back of the seat. She was tired. He said after a minute, "You'll miss Ede."

"Yes."

He tried again. He said, "Jenny, the other night when I was taking you home from the office —"

"I'd forgotten," she said.

"No, and you can't put me off that way. Would you marry me if I wrote Andrea and asked her to divorce me on her return? She might, you know. In fact, I don't see why she wouldn't. She doesn't want me," he said bitterly. "As to my father's objections, they don't matter much, now," he said.

"Why?" asked Jenny bluntly.

"Oh," he said, shrugging, "a lot of reasons. Perhaps one is purely financial. I've more money of my own," he said carelessly, "than I used to have —"

How? Jenny asked herself. She inquired no further. What was the use? But a great deal of money passed through Justice's hands these days. She thought, So the reason he didn't want to be divorced before was, he was afraid he'd be cut off or something.

He said urgently, "We could be very happy, I think. You're — a pretty remarkable little person. I don't know why, exactly."

She said, "Neither do I."

Justice said, "You haven't answered me."

She asked, "Is it usual to ask a girl to marry you before you're divorced?"

"Quite," he said. "What a funny little creature you are, darling."

"It's unusual," she said thoughtfully, "in Seahaven. How would you put it? Mrs. Newton announces the engagement of her granddaughter provided that her granddaughter's fiancé's wife will consent to a divorce in the remote future? Well," said

Jenny, "isn't that wonderful!"

He said angrily, "But I'm in love with you!"

"That's wonderful too," said Jenny. She added, sitting up, "and you have learned somehow that I'm not interested in cocktails at the Ritz or Copley Plaza, or a weekend at —"

He said, "Be quiet."

She said evenly, "You don't want to marry me, Justice."

He said angrily, "It's Steve Barton, I suppose . . . although you've denied it and denied it."

"Denied what?"

"That you're in love with him."

"I don't remember denying it," she said thoughtfully. Had she, had she not? She sat up again, so straight and so suddenly, that he jumped. She asked, startled, "Justice, do you suppose I am . . . that I've been all along?"

"What?" he demanded, bewildered.

"In love with Steve? Of course, I was when I was a kid, but I hadn't thought of him that way in years. Or . . . had I? I don't know, I'm all mixed up. And when he came back he was so changed and we quarreled —"

He said, "This is a charming situation. Am

I explaining you to yourself? Well, if you are in love with him, forget it. I fancy Mary has other plans for him."

She said, "Oh, Mary. I'd forgotten her too," and lapsed into silence.

She thought, He's right of course. I am in love with Steve. I've always loved him. That isn't being in love, of course. But now . . .

She said firmly, "She shan't have him."

"Why not?" asked Justice. "If she wants him and he's agreeable."

"Oh," said Jenny, "Steve doesn't belong . . . any more than I would. We're both just too Seahaven," she said.

"I could shake you," said Justice, "and you aren't in love with Dr. Barton. You couldn't talk about it, this way, if you were. Not to me, anyway. I don't understand you," he told her, "which makes you ten per cent more exciting. You are exciting, you know."

She said serenely, "Am I? I thought that in order to be exciting a gal had to have glamour — the slink and sleek type. Not my type," she said modestly.

"I," said Justice, "have had about enough of this."

He pulled the car off the road, stopped it, leaned over and scooped Jenny closer to him. He kissed her, very effectively.

Jenny said, extricating herself, "I ought to slap your face!"

He said, "That gesture went out in the early nineteen hundreds."

"Not in Seahaven," said Jenny, and slapped him hard.

Justice blinked and then he laughed. He said, and set the car in motion again, "The prosecution rests, darling. But I'm going to write Andrea."

"Give her," said Jenny, "my regards."

When the car stopped at the Newtons', Justice spoke. He said, "I have to trek back to New York tomorrow, I think . . . but you aren't rid of me, Jenny. I don't give up easily. I'll be around . . . and I'll be seeing you, baby."

"Wolf, wolf," said Jenny sweetly. She got out of the car and he made no move to aid or to stop her. She paused, her hand on the door. She said, "I'll expect you then, huffing and puffing."

She went into the house, laughing, heard the car drive off, and found Ede and Gram in Ede's room sorting things to be packed. Ede had just come in a few moments before. Gram said, looking up from her work, "Oh, there you are, Jenny. Steve came in. He wanted to see you, he was sorry to have missed you."

Jenny said, yawning, "We tore over to Northam like a couple of bats out of hell."

"Jenifer!"

"Well, approximately," she said, unabashed. "Butch, come here. Stop bedeviling Uncle Rafe, you've worn all the fur off the back of his neck carting him around like that. . . . Anyway," she went on, "we took the message to Garcia straight to the train where it was received by a very handsome man, and whisked off to Washington. I'd like to go to Washington," said Jenny dreamily, "and tiptoe midst the cherry blossoms."

Ede said, "You're up to something, isn't she, Gram?"

Gram regarded Jenny over her spectacles. She said mildly, "She sounds as usual, a little high-strung and incoherent."

Jenny sat down on the bed. She didn't look at Ede. She said, "Gram, I've news."

"Such as?" asked Gram cautiously.

"Mr. Hathaway," said Jenny, "proposed to me tonight. That is to say, he suggested that if Mrs. Hathaway would give him a divorce, we might be very happy together. He didn't mention the lush surroundings, and the surtaxes . . . but they're all there, darling."

Gram's fine skin flushed with shock and anger, and Jenny glanced at Ede, who was looking white and a little sick.

Gram said, and her voice shook, "Jenifer Newton, if you aren't making this up!"

"I'm not," said Jenny.

"Then," said Gram, "it's indecent. And you're to resign at once. And, moreover, you must have encouraged him."

"Well," said Jenny pacifically, "not lately, at all events. But I'm not going to resign, Gram, not until I find a job as good or better. I think Mr. Hathaway is just a little bored. He doesn't want to marry me, or anyone," she said rapidly, "but I'm handy. A peg on which to hang his manly emotions, like a hat. Maybe a pair of antlers. Anyway, I refused, without thanks. We are good friends and no hard feelings, I hope."

Ede released her breath, which apparently she had been holding. But Gram was not appeased.

She said, "It's disgusting. A young girl and a married man!"

"Darling," said Jenny, "hold your horses."

Gram looked at Ede. She said, "I want to talk to Jenny alone."

Ede spoke for the first time. She said, "Okay, I'm going down to get a glass of milk anyway."

"Bring me one," said Jenny, swinging her

251

little feet, "and six filled cookies, if you can find them. I'm starved."

When the door had shut, Gram looked at Jenny.

"I don't understand you," she said.

"That's good," said Jenny. "But I haven't been up to anything, Gram."

"But men don't — without encouragement . . ." Gram began.

Jenny said thoughtfully, "I did think he was pretty superior, at first. Oh, I wasn't serious about him, just sort of swoon-Sinatra. It was fan stuff. You know, front row, and won't you please send me your autograph. But I became disillusioned at about the time he became interested."

Gram said, "I remember you told me once that you thought you were headed for trouble."

"This is it," said Jenny.

Gram asked gravely, "Jenny, was it because of Ede?"

It was Jenny's turn to lose color. She answered, breathlessly, "I don't know what you mean, Gram."

"After Ede heard about Dick," said Gram, "she was so miserable those first few days that she said something to me. Not much. But I put two and two together. I realized that she was reproaching herself for — something. Was it Justice Hathaway?"

Jenny said quickly, "Ede's exaggeration. It was just a silly flirtation." There was a word, she reflected, Gram would recognize and understand. "That's all. She was lonely, and she kept going to the Hathaway house and he was there."

Gram said, "So I gathered." She smiled but the tears were bright in her eyes. Jenny thought, Ede said more than she meant to and poor little Gram's been thinking and worrying . . . and wondering.

She said, "There wasn't anything to it, dear. I suppose she sort of magnified everything to herself. Anyway, I went all over noble and sisterly and made myself as agreeable to the boss as possible. I thought I could divert him, a sort of minor booby trap. I was pretty surprised when it blew up in my face with a proposal tonight. It was silly of me."

"Silly," said Gram, "indiscreet and unnecessary. Ede would have come to her senses without your help. She's a Newton," said Gram, with pride. "She wouldn't let herself down — nor us."

"Of course not," said Jenny.

Gram rose. "I hear her coming," she said. She put her hand on Jenny's shoulder. "I wish you would try and find another position, Jenny. I don't like this situation at all," she added.

Jenny said meekly, "I'll try, Gram."

When Gram had gone and Ede had returned, the two girls drank their milk companionably. Ede said, "You gave me a shock. I suppose you intended to."

"Well, in a way," said Jenny, "just in case you —"

Ede said harshly, "I know. I wish Gram hadn't been here, though."

"It was the only way to make you believe it, telling you in front of her," said Jenny.

"It couldn't make any difference. If you knew how I despise myself."

Jenny said humbly, "I just wanted you to know that I — well, I was playing red herring."

Ede smiled shakily. "I've known that," she said, "for some time. You are an idiot, darling." She leaned over to take Jenny's hand. "I'll miss you a lot." She added, "But you're in pretty deep with Gram."

"Gram," said Jenny, "will tell me I'm climbing fool's hill, and she's right."

"What do you intend to do?"

"Stick," said Jenny. "He won't bother me, Ede. He knows when he's licked."

"But suppose," said Ede, "he does ask for a divorce?"

"Then," said Jenny promptly, "I'll bet Mrs. H. comes home running, either by submarine or by bomber. And once he sees her again, he'll forget I ever existed."

Chapter Sixteen

Mrs. Hathaway was coming home, not because her husband had written her but because she had not been well for some time and her superiors decided that she needed a long rest, after which she could be useful in her own country. She cabled that she was coming, she did not know just when, but they might shortly expect her.

Steve was at the Hathaway house when Mary, opening the cable, telephoned Justice in New York. They were in the library looking at the final plans which were to be presented at the town meeting. They were good plans, but would of course have to be greatly modified. He thought, That can be remedied, in good time and by the right people. He had plans of his own — if they went through.

Mary hung up, and turned. She said, "This is pretty exciting news — not that I've ever cared much for my esteemed sister-in-law. Although I admire her, as who wouldn't." She looked at him thoughtfully. "She would have made you a wonderful wife, Steve, if she were a little younger, and hadn't met Justice first. She has beauty, poise, common sense, intelligence — and money."

"Well, thanks," said Steve politely.

"Also," said Mary, "she isn't frivolous. Poor Justice." She sat down on the edge of the big table and regarded him. She said, "You are a difficult man."

"A simple one," said Steve firmly.

Mary said, after a moment, "We could have had a good deal of fun together, Steve, with sparkle in it."

"Four dry Martinis have sparkle too," said Steve, "and create a hell of a hangover."

Her face tightened. She said, and touched the papers on the desk, "You realize I could persuade my father to drop all this?"

"I don't think so."

"There are ways," said Mary. "He trusts me, far more than Justice, for instance. If I said that it would cost much more than we thought originally . . ."

"He isn't a child," said Steve.

She said gently, "I didn't mean money, exactly. If I pointed out that immortalizing the Hathaway name might not be the road to the hearts of the stiff-necked Seahaveners."

"He's vain," said Steve, "he won't believe you."

"I might suggest," said Mary, "that *you* aren't in this for reasons of pure humanitarianism."

"You could," said Steve, "suggest a lot of things. But the hospital will go through, one way or another."

She was silent. Then she said, "Justice may not be happy at Andrea's sudden appearance."

"No?" asked Steve politely.

"No," said Mary. "He has other fish to fry. . . . Not, I think, as cold," she added thoughtfully.

Steve looked a little grim. He asked, "Why not say you mean Jenny?"

"Well," Mary said, "if you want to take it up where we left it, the other night."

"I don't."

Mary said, "You might be interested in knowing that he has dreams of domesticity. He came in the other night — it appeared they had driven to Northam together on an alleged emergency errand — you would have thought the War and Navy Departments were sitting around a large table in Washington, sending out couriers and carrier pigeons. Anyway, he came in all pepped up. He had two highballs and told me that he wished Andrea would divorce him. He'd like to settle down to a normal life, build a home, raise a family. That was, of course, a slap in the face for Andrea. She couldn't hear or feel it, naturally, but he was thinking of her — and of Jenny."

"And why Jenny?"

"It's obvious. Jenny has old-fashioned ideas. She plays for keeps. Apparently my little brother got that through his beautiful head and it intrigued him. He's been used to other games."

Steve rose and stood looking at her. He said, "You're a pretty woman, Mary, with a very ugly mind."

She was white with anger but she said steadily, "Thanks, too much."

He walked over and took her by the shoulders. He said, "No, I'm the one who owes you gratitude. You've helped me a lot, in more ways than one. And I'm not unmindful of it."

"Joseph?" she inquired.

"I know. It's a role few men like to play. Makes 'em feel damned silly. Potiphar's wife was very attractive," said Steve, with half a sigh, "likewise persistent. Also," he added calmly, "obvious. Yet, I am grateful. You see, I didn't like myself when I came home. I didn't like what was left of me, body and mind, nor the sort of life I'd have to adjust myself to, nor the fact that my friends knew and were sorry for me. You weren't. You were tough about it. That was good for me, good psychology for any man as self-pitying as I was. That rates gratitude. Also you made it plain that you, at least, did not find me repellent. Which was very good for what is termed my morale. Then, too, you got me interested in something besides myself. The hospital. And in addition, Madam Potiphar, you opened my eyes to a number of interesting and personal things."

"How very girl scout," said Mary.

"Exactly." He picked her up, and set her on her feet with astonishing ease. Even his bad arm had strength. He kissed her, lightly, at the corner of her mouth. "That's for good-bye," he said.

"Good-bye?"

"I think so . . . for a while anyway. I'll see you at the town meeting." He went to the door, and turned. He said gently, "You're not such a bad kid after all, not nearly so bad as you think you are and try to be. I'll bet you make Howard Morgan a damned good wife. I'm a little sorry I have to — well, do what I must. Sorry, I mean, for your sake. Not for anyone else's." His face was hard at the moment. Then it softened, and he grinned. He said, "Well, as far as you and I are concerned, no harm done. See you later." He flipped his left hand at her in a gesture of farewell, and was gone.

Mary stood looking after him. Her heart was tight. What had he meant, and why? She thought forlornly, I don't really love him, I don't suppose I'll ever love anyone but Pat, damn him. And still —

She didn't think he had meant it, saying good-bye like that. If he did, there was always Howard. She was sick of men, she told herself angrily.

She looked down at the plans a moment, threw them on the floor and rang for cocktails. No use waiting until the regular hour. Steve had gone.

She thought, I must have a talk with Jenny.

The next day, when Justice was still in New York, Mary came into the office and asked, "Interrupting you, Jenny?"

Jenny said, "No," politely and took her hands off the keys.

Mary walked around the little room. She asked, "When's Ede going?"

"Monday."

"I hope she'll be happy," said Mary. She came up to the desk, and smiled. She wore a white tweed suit and a high-necked black cashmere sweater. She carried a black bag, and wore sheer stockings — nylons, thought Jenny, sighing — and black suède shoes. She was very tanned and her lipstick was brilliant. She asked, "Aren't you excited about the hospital?"

Jenny nodded. She said, "It's what we've always needed."

"It will be splendid for Steve," said Mary. "Of course, you know, he's a very clever guy. Too clever to be mewed up in a little dump like this."

"He's needed, too," Jenny said.

"I dare say." Mary shrugged. "But it seems too bad. He's had a chance to get out, make something of himself. He could have a very fine practice, with the right backing."

"Meaning?" asked Jenny.

"Me," said Mary, and smiled.

Jenny raised her eyes and looked at her. She asked slowly, "You — and Steve?"

Mary shrugged. She said casually, "Don't jump to conclusions. But I could help him, if he could be persuaded to leave Seahaven."

Jenny asked, "And the hospital?"

"I fancy," said Mary, "it would function without him." At the door, she said, "You'd heard that Andrea is coming home? Perhaps she's decided on a retake. In any case, discretion is indicated until Justice learns whether she intends to call it a day, or until death do them part. I just thought you'd like to know."

"Thanks," said Jenny, breathing a little hard, her color high.

After Mary left, she picked up a pencil and drew doodles. Some were fierce round cats with whiskers; others, skinny little devils with pitchforks. She thought, Well, what was that about? So Seahaven is holding Steve back from a great career. Nuts, Jenny informed herself, his career's right here. She doesn't intend to marry him — even if he'd say yes, Jenny thought, with an irrepressible giggle, but if he decided to hang up his shingle in New York, she could send him all the Best People. And he'd be so grateful. It's a pretty picture. As for Justice, I'm to play mousie . . . And that's quaint too.

Andrea Hathaway returned by clipper and Justice met her at the field. They went directly to his father's apartment and Mr. Hathaway was pathetically happy to see his daughter-in-law. She was the one person in the world for whom he had entire respect and selfless affection. On the following day they came to Seahaven, arriving in the evening, and the next morning when Justice came to the office Andrea was with him.

They walked in, and Jenny looked up, startled, from her work and rose. Andrea was a much too slender woman, and her face was haggard. She had such distinction that you did not notice her clothes. You saw only the fine, clear bone structure, and the candid, luminous and friendly eyes. Justice made the presentations, and Andrea put her hand in Jenny's. A few moments later she looked at her husband gravely. She said, "Run along, Justice, I want to speak to Jenny."

He looked anxious and sheepish, his poise evaporating. Andrea smiled. She looked younger then, her face illuminated. She said gently, "Don't worry."

He said, with awkward heartiness, "Okay, I'll leave you girls to yourselves," and went into his office and shut the door. Andrea sat down on the straight chair by the desk and looked at Jenny. She said, "Justice has told me about you."

Jenny said, "There isn't much to tell."

Andrea smiled. She said, "Don't be on the defensive, my dear. You're very young, and pretty — and untouched. After Justice met me, we had a long talk. He said, at once, that he had become interested in someone else. And so, he wished a divorce."

"But," said Jenny, scarlet, "I don't want.

. . . that is, I haven't —"

"I know," said Andrea mildly. "He admitted that you had refused to consider marrying him in the event of a divorce. I came here to ask you something. Are you in love with him? Is it because of — me that you refuse? Now that I've seen you I realize that it might be," she added. "I wasn't sure at first."

Jenny shook her head, with violence. The sun danced on her hair and it seemed to Andrea that sparks flew. She said, "Mrs. Hathaway, please believe me, I'm not in love with him; I wouldn't marry him if he had never had a wife! When I first came to work for him, I — well, gosh," said Jenny, "you know how it is. Big shot, glamour, and all that. It wasn't serious, it was just fun, it made the work easier and as far as he was concerned he didn't know I was alive. And then," she added soberly, "when he did, I —" she looked at Andrea directly — "I wasn't having any. Not on account of you," she added hardily, "although of course it should have been. It was just . . . the way I felt . . . and because," she told Andrea, "there's someone else."

"I see." Andrea was quiet. Then she said, "I came back to ask Justice if he wanted to try again. Much of our unhappiness has been my fault. I was deeply in love when we were married. I had, also, very high standards, and I was neither tolerant nor patient. He's — volatile, gay. He likes excitement, and women. Half of it's the chase," she added. "I wasn't old enough or wise enough to meet the situation. I read all sorts of meanings into flirtations. They weren't affairs. He was just —" She broke off. "There were scenes," she said. "And then when my baby was born I transferred all my affection, I believed he would be compensation — I didn't think Justice worth my misery. I promised myself that I would find my happiness in my child. I don't believe that —" she hesitated, spoke painfully — "that my husband was unfaithful to me, actually, until then. When I knew, I told myself I didn't care."

She paused. Then she went on unevenly:

"When my little boy died, nothing seemed to matter, Justice least of all. I blamed him for the tragedy. It was stupid and quite unfair. When I went to England it was with the idea of putting as much distance between us as possible and of not returning. Then the war came. I went through the blitz. I saw such suffering and courage as I had never believed possible . . . I saw utterly unselfish devotion, I saw people rise above horror and grief and agony. And I felt so small, so petty.

It had all been my ego, Jenny. I had thought of myself as a good woman. I had felt that I possessed a superior sort of nobility. But what I experienced in England made me aware of myself. I realized that, all along, I had been merely jealous and possessive. I had loved my son, yes, but part of that love was an attempt to hurt his father. So when I found I must return I determined to ask my husband if we could go on again. On a different, more honest basis. But when I learned about you I had to know —" She broke off. She said, "Why, you're *crying!*"

Jenny said shakily, "I'm being silly, but I can't help it." She added, "Please, Mrs. Hathaway, I never for an instant —" She tried to smile. "I hope you'll be so happy," she ended.

"It may not be what you'd call happiness," said Andrea thoughtfully, "but I shall try. If . . ." She sighed. "That's the catch, isn't it?" she murmured. She rose, put out her hand and took Jenny's. "I'm glad he hasn't hurt you. But if you never loved him, naturally, he couldn't. Jenny, I'd like to adopt two small children. I can't have any of my own. But if we adopted them, a boy and a girl — ?"

Jenny rose. She said, "I do hope so."

Andrea smiled. "Thank you, Jenny."

Jenny watched her go into Justice's office and shut the door. She sat down and tried to work, took page after page from her type-writer and threw them into the wastebasket. And a paper shortage too, she told herself crossly.

She thought, He isn't worth her little fin-ger, but I don't suppose that makes any difference. And she's always cared for him, no matter what she thought.

It seemed a long time before they came out of the office. Justice was smiling but he looked like a man who has had a severe shock. Andrea was grave. It was her habit to be grave, Jenny surmised, but there was a warmth in her regard that was better than smiling. Justice stopped and looked at Jenny. He said, "If anyone calls, I'm taking the day off. Andrea and I are going to look at houses."

"Fine," said Jenny, and gave him her open smile, that of a good child.

The door closed behind them. She told herself, I'll go on working here, everything will be swell. They aren't going to live at the big house, they'll find a place of their own and work this out together. She thought again, I don't think he's worth it, but if she does . . . well, that's okay with me.

She did not see them again that day. At

supper she reported to Gram and Ede. She said, "Mrs. Hathaway's here. I met her this morning. She's pretty remarkable."

"What does she look like?" asked Ede unwillingly.

"Oh, I don't know," said Jenny vaguely, "like her pictures, I suppose, only more so. She has the loveliest hands and voice and her eyes look right into you . . ."

Ede said, with an effort, "Sounds terrifying. What did she wear?"

"I haven't," said Jenny, "the least idea. They went out to look for a house. I guess they're going to settle down here. But not up at the big place." She looked at Ede. "She wants to adopt two children," she said.

Ede asked after a moment, "They've made it up?"

"That's right," said Jenny.

She thought, How long will it last, how long will he try to live up to her, if he does try? Maybe forever. Maybe all the shopping around at bargain counters was his way of compensating. Maybe he'd be satisfied now. You couldn't know. She hoped so, for Andrea's sake. She thought, She'll stand by him this time.

She saw Andrea next at the town meeting, which took place a few nights after Ede left for California. They had seen her off. Jenny and Gram, a few of Ede's closest friends, Steve, and Mary Hathaway. Ede had flowers to take with her, books, candy. Standing on the platform, she had looked pretty and anxious and excited. Jenny could hardly see her, for the foolish tears. She thought, She's going so far, and she may not like it. But she will, after she sees Dick again. She squeezed Gram's hand, hard, and ran to put her arms around her sister, to kiss her once more before the conductor signaled and called, "All aboard —"

And Ede said, low, "Don't worry. I'll be all right. I can wait for Dick now. I feel that it won't be long before I see him, and we are together again for good. And it will be for good, I promise you."

The train pulled out, and Steve took Jenny and Gram home. Before he got into the car, Mary detained him. She talked to him for a moment, low, urgently, and he listened, saying little. Jenny saw him shake his head. She heard him say, "It's no good, Mary."

Driving back he was silent. Once he roused himself to ask, "You're surely coming to the meeting? Suppose I stop for you . . . I hope to heaven I'm not called away."

Jenny said, "You sound as if you intended to make a speech."

"Well," he said, "something of the sort.

270

Maybe I should keep my mouth shut and take what the gods — or the Hathaways — bestow." He was silent as Jenny cried, "What on earth do you mean, Steve?" but said only, "You'll see."

Chapter Seventeen

The Town Hall was old, it was frame, and part of it dated back to the Revolution. The big room was crowded. The selectmen sat in their accustomed places, and the clerk. And the moderator presided.

The Hathaways were there, en masse. Horace looking pleased with himself, and Mary, with Howard Morgan, Andrea with Justice. They sat by themselves, to the left, in the front row. Jenny waved at them. The Richards were there, of course, and practically everyone else . . . Dr. Mathews was there and Dr. Brown and Dr. Peters, Judge Fawcett, Higgins and Perkins the leading lawyers, all the leading merchants . . . well, just about everybody.

Foster, the architect, was there, too. Mr. Hathaway had summoned him from Portland.

It was Mr. Hathaway who did the speaking. His own lawyer was with him, appearing suddenly from the back of the room and seating himself beside Foster. Mr. Hathaway was impressive. He said that he supposed by now that everyone present had heard of the proposed hospital. He had with him the plans, and the architect. He could tell the townspeople how much it would cost to build and endow. He wished to give it to the town as a symbol of the pleasure he had found there. He added, "and the profit." He felt it only right that much of the proceeds of the yard should be returned to the town. He spoke briefly of future organization, the board of directors which would be elected to oversee the hospital. He spoke kindly of Steve — the son of one of the most respected citizens of Seahaven — who would work there together with the other doctors now in Seahaven and those who would eventually return from the war, and others who would come from other towns and settle here because of new opportunities.

When, finally, he sat down there was a great deal of applause. And then Foster spoke, at some length, from the floor. After which the moderator asked for a discussion.

Jenny felt Steve tense beside her, but he did not move until a number of people had risen to applaud Mr. Hathaway's generosity and civic concern. When the last, a large lady, clad in a somewhat astonishing foulard — she was president of the women's aide and the garden club — had finished, Steve rose. He spoke from where he stood, as was the custom, very simply.

He said, "I think we should be clear on a number of things. One is, if Mr. Hathaway's offer is accepted, how far, and how completely, would he, and his chosen board, expect to dictate the hospital policies."

There was a slight murmur among the audience. The moderator looked somewhat shocked. Mr. Hathaway rose, delicate shade of mauve suffusing his face. He said, "I object to the word 'dictate.' "

"How far?" asked Steve evenly.

Hathaway said, after a moment, "Naturally I would expect to take a very active interest."

Steve nodded. "I thought so. I have been talking to Dr. Mathews, to Dr. Brown and Dr. Peters. Also to others of our townspeople. We may be in the minority but we feel that, generous as is Mr. Hathaway's offer, the town should not accept it." He waited until the stir had died down. Then he went on: "Seahaven is prosperous enough to build and support its own hospital. This could not be built on such elaborate and costly lines as Mr. Hathaway's. It would have to be smaller, and to expand only when we could afford it. It would not be planned, as now, as an institution comprising mostly private rooms, with only one small charity ward and one semiprivate. It would have a few private rooms, but would be largely for semiprivate and ward patients. We could concentrate upon the best modern equipment, rather than outward show — elaborate waiting rooms, for instance, and the expensive landscaping. Landscaping comes later. What we need is a hospital that will provide adequately and at low cost for our patients."

Hathaway rose. He said, "I want no part of socialized medicine."

Steve said gently, as the murmur rose and died, "I am not proposing socialized medicine. I am proposing care for those who need it, at the lowest practical cost. Private rooms, yes, but not a hospital composed of them. Moreover, there must be adequate funds for clinics and for the care of veterans discharged from the services, who need care . . . particularly in the neuropsychiatric field . . . for whom there is no other provision."

Hathaway was still standing. He said, apoplectic, "I cannot conceive that Seahaven would seriously consider refusing my offer. Where would the town get the money?"

Steve said, raising his voice, "From the people, Mr. Hathaway. In dollar bills, five-dollar bills. From the people who can afford a little and those who can afford more.

From the bank, which believes in its depositors. Seahaven has always more than filled its quota in any other important project whether Community Chest or Red Cross or War Bonds. It will do so now. It will take time, but it can be done."

Hathaway cried, "That's nonsense! You spoke of Seahaven being prosperous, Dr. Barton. You must admit that its prosperity stems from the shipyard."

"Granted," said Steve cheerfully, "but first of all from the physical labor of the people who work there. You can't run an industry without people. And there is money in Seahaven," he said, "which was there long before the yards changed hands."

Hathaway said furiously, "I think we should put this to a vote, Mr. Moderator."

"Just a minute," said Steve. He looked across the room at Hathaway. "I think it would interest the people here if they knew that the Hathaway interests, under another name and through various holding companies, own and, through their employees, operate the new roadside places in Seahaven, including the one known as the Barnacle. And not in Seahaven alone, as that would be hardly worthwhile, but along the entire coast line of the state, and also in the interior . . ."

There was immediate confusion. A woman cried out and Jenny, breathless, incredulous, knew without turning her head that it was the mother of one of the youngsters who had been injured in the fire. Mr. Hathaway's lawyer rose and tried to make himself heard through the clamor. No one heard anything he said except . . . "quite beside the point."

Steve spoke, and when he did so, people became quiet. "It isn't beside the point," he said. "Seahaven might feel that Mr. Hathaway's offer was made by way of making secret amends. But it wasn't. The offer was made before the fire. The offer was made" — Jenny could have sworn that he looked at Mary and smiled a little — "mainly to perpetuate the name of Hathaway."

Someone spoke, rising from his chair. He said, "Mr. Hathaway hasn't made any statement or a denial of his connection with those places."

Steve said, "He can't. I have the evidence. It took me some time to get it. I have evidence that a number of these places sell liquor to minors and commit other infractions of the law. I have evidence of bribery, paid to members of the police force, and to fire inspectors. It is all in the hands of Mr. Higgins, the attorney. It has nothing to do with the present discussion, but will be produced in court later when the Barnacle trial comes up. Meantime we are concerned with the projected hospital. Does Seahaven want a hospital built, managed, and named by the Hathaway interests or has it sufficient self-respect to dig down into its own pockets and produce the money necessary to build one which will be a Seahaven institution, managed and planned by the people who build it?"

The uproar was incredible. Gram kept striking her little palms together, and her eyes snapped. She was saying, "Good for you, Steve." And Jenny, as Steve sat down and wiped his forehead, put her hand over his. She said, "Steve, you're pretty wonderful."

He was on their side, and had been all along. He was his father's son.

It was late when the meeting was dismissed. Seahaven had voted against the Hathaway hospital. Seahaven was going to build its own. Committees were elected to look into plans, to consider financing, to raise money by various means, by publication, subscriptions, and gatherings as well as by borrowing.

And someone jumped up and cried, "There's only one name for this hospital. It should be named for the man who always wanted one, and who was bitterly disappointed because we didn't come up to scratch. It should be named for Bert Barton!"

Before that, Horace Hathaway had hurried to his car, with Foster and the lawyer. But Mary waited on the hall steps, and in the background were Justice and Andrea. Mary spoke to Steve, coming out with Gram and Jenny, surrounded by excited and talkative people. Seahaven hadn't known such excitement in years. She said, "I suppose you think you're very clever and heroic."

"Nope," he said.

She said, "I won't forgive you, and anything we can do to —"

"To discredit me," he said, "you'll do. It can't matter, Mary, I never had a fancy practice."

She said, "You're just a small-town plodder, after all."

"That's all," he agreed. "And you," he said, "you knew about the Hathaway juke boxes, didn't you?" He laughed. "Pretty small pickings, or wasn't it?"

She turned, with Morgan beside her, and went down the steps. But Justice stepped forward and held out his hand. He said, "We deserved that, Steve. Would your committees accept some tainted money, without strings to it, from me? Not very tainted. Not, in any event, concerned with — real estate."

"Sure," said Steve, "we'll accept it." He looked at Andrea with interest and Andrea said, smiling, "Justice forgot the amenities, Dr. Barton. I'm Andrea Hathaway. We're buying a house on the Country Club Road, and we hope you'll come to see us, you and," she smiled again, "Jenny."

They sat in Gram's kitchen and Gram poured the coffee and got out the doughnuts. They had talked and talked, the three of them. And Gram said, "I like the look of Mr. Hathaway's wife."

Jenny said, "She'll be your fancy practice, Steve, you'll see. No matter what Horace may say or do." She hugged herself as far as she could reach. "It was marvelous." She sighed. "It all works out. I get a new job — for Horace's sake, and you get your hospital and I bet a cooky Horace moves back to New York or wherever and Mary with him. I bet they'll sell the house if Justice doesn't want it. And I don't think he does. Because Andrea won't."

Steve said, "You know all about them, don't you?"

"I think so."

Gram was yawning. "It's been a big evening . . . I'll leave you two to talk it over," and scurried out of the room, smiling to herself.

The clock ticked and Butch, waiting for Jenny to go upstairs, purred. And Steve asked, "You aren't sore?"

"Me? Why should I be?"

He said, "I don't know, now that Mrs. Hathaway's back. But you might be."

She said gravely, "Steve, I wanted to tell you before. It — never meant anything. I wasn't in love with him. I just got scared . . . about Ede. I thought if I threw myself at him, he might, well, catch me up, and it would prove to Ede that practically any girl who wasn't repulsive could get him. That was all, Steve, honestly."

He said, "I know. Ede told me, the night she left for California."

He made a long arm and drew her to him. He said, "I've been waiting for you to grow up. I didn't know it until recently. How are my chances? Are you in love with anyone, Jenny?"

"Yes, I'm in love with you. Oh, Steve . . ."

He held her close then, and kissed her. It wasn't the first time, but it was different.

She said contentedly, "I suppose we'll fight like anything."

"Of course . . . I love you so much. And you're crazy."

"You too, Steve, it won't be easy, bucking Horace Hathaway. He'll do all he can to stop you."

"Not too much," said Steve. "He doesn't like having Seahaven know his side deals. The Barnacle, for instance. . . . Jenny, how much do you love me?"

"I don't know," she said. "I dare say it isn't as much as it will be when we're old and tottering. It's the sort of love that will keep on growing."

The telephone rang and Jenny went to answer it. She called, "It's for you, darling," and Gram, peeking over the top of the stair, heard and went back to her room. She thought, And now it will be all right. She thought, I'll hate giving up this house — I won't, we'll rent it, I'll leave it to Jenny — but I suppose Steve will want to go on living in Bert's. Because she would live with them, the rest of her days, wherever they lived. She knew that.

It was Mattie. Steve took the message, and hung up. "It's a call," he said, and swept Jenny into his arms. "You see what it's going to be like, married to a general practitioner? I haven't kissed you enough, I haven't said . . ."

She said, "Being a general practitioner's wife is all I want, Steve, as long as you're the G.P. and we have all our lives to kiss, and to talk."

She went to the door with him, and as it closed and she heard the engine start she thought, Well, I wasn't out of a job very long, was I?

Running upstairs to burst in on Gram, to cry, "Steve and I are going to be married, just as soon as we can," she thought, A life job . . . and the only one worthwhile.

She knocked on Gram's door, and opened it. "Gram," she said, "the most wonderful thing has happened!"

The employees of Thorndike Press hope you have enjoyed this Large Print book. All our Large Print titles are designed for easy reading, and all our books are made to last. Other Thorndike Press Large Print books are available at your library, through selected bookstores, or directly from us.

For information about titles, please call:

(800) 223-2336

To share your comments, please write:

Publisher
Thorndike Press
P.O. Box 159
Thorndike, Maine 04986